BOUNTY ON A BARON

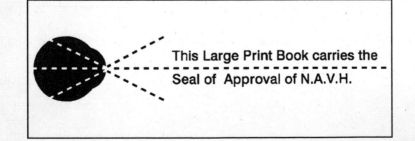

BOUNTY ON A BARON

ROBERT J. RANDISI

WHEELER PUBLISHING
A part of Gale, Cengage Learning

GALE
CENGAGE Learning·

Detroit • New York • San Francisco • New Haven, Conn • Waterville, Maine • London

GALE
CENGAGE Learning™

LIBRARY OF CONGRESS CATALOGING-IN-PUBLICATION DATA

Randisi, Robert J.
    Bounty on a baron / by Robert J. Randisi.
        p. cm. — (Wheeler Publishing large print western)
    ISBN-13: 978-1-4104-2602-4 (alk. paper)
    ISBN-10: 1-4104-2602-5 (alk. paper)
    1. Bounty hunters—Fiction. 2. Large type books. I. Title.
PS3568.A53B68 2010
813'.54—dc22   2010003205

Published in 2010 by arrangement with Dominick Abel Literary Agency, Inc.

Printed in the United States of America
1 2 3 4 5 6 7 14 13 12 11 10

To Ed Gorman

Prologue I

Kendall, Wyoming

They called him "the Baron," and that's exactly what he was, a bon-i-fidey Baron, from Russia. He never talked about it, though, not to anybody. It was a painful memory, fleeing Russia to escape his enemies, coming to the United States without a penny to his name. He tried working at different jobs, but none of them ever paid off. So, he turned to what he knew best.

Killing.

Even in Russia he had been a hired killer, but it was done differently there. Killing was killing, but he'd had to learn the new trappings that surrounded his profession in America.

In Russia, a rifle had been his weapon, and a knife. In America, he had to learn how to use a handgun, and he found that he had a natural talent with it. He had speed, he had accuracy. It soon became as natural as pointing his finger — the way it was with all the good ones.

He also needed a new name to go with everything else. Keeping the old one would allow his enemies to track him down too easily — even in this far-away country. He decided to use Brand — he liked the way it sounded. The first time he'd heard the word in the American West it had been something you did to a steer. Now it was his name.

Then there was his accent. Hard as he tried, he couldn't lose it completely. It became more pronounced whenever he tried to speak quickly, so to counteract that, he rarely spoke unless it was absolutely necessary —

Like now.

"Outside," he said to Stu Carver.

Carver turned and looked at him, and so did the other men in the saloon. There were about half a dozen but the Baron had eyes only for Carver.

"The Baron," Stu Carver said, the two words a terrified whisper.

No one knew about the Baron's background, but during the three years since he'd started his new life many people had commented on how regal his bearing always was. Some men even said he acted like royalty. Like a king or a duke or a baron, somebody had said. The name "Baron" stuck, even though he had never called himself anything but "Brand."

Now, Carver was no coward, but when he saw the Baron standing there his blood ran cold and his stomach did flip-flops. There was only one reason the Baron came to town — and he had called Carver's name.

"Me?" Carver said.

The Baron nodded.

"But, why me?"

The Baron shrugged. He had never asked why before taking a job, and he never intended to. It didn't matter to him.

"Listen —" Stu Carver said, standing up.

"Outside."

If it was avoidable, Brand liked to kill his man without taking anyone else with him. Extra killings brought in no recompense.

Carver had two friends in the saloon, and they straightened up now. Brand saw them but did not make a move.

"Outside," he said for the third time, then backed out of the saloon into the darkness.

Carver came out of the saloon first, sweating. He was followed by his two friends, who fanned out on either side.

"Baron?" Carver called.

"Step away from the light."

It was good advice, but it wasn't meant to

be. Brand didn't want any stray shots going into the saloon and hitting some innocent bystander.

The three men stepped into the street, and Brand walked into a shaft of moonlight.

They all drew and fired.

Carver fired in haste and missed. Brand's shot took him square in the chest. Brand never fired in haste.

Carver's two friends fired several shots, but Brand leaped quickly to the left and heard the bullets whiz by him. He calmly squeezed off two more shots and then the whole town seemed to grow quiet.

He walked over and checked the bodies, Carver's last.

"Damned waste," he said. He'd been paid to kill one man, and he'd killed three. That was wasted lead for him.

He heard a noise behind him, then. Spinning around, he drew and fired. A man fell dead, and Brand went over to check the body. Carver must have sent someone out a back window, he thought. He knew the saloon had no back door.

Using his foot, he turned the body over. A muscle in his jaw began to jump when he saw that he'd killed a boy. Big for his age, but probably no more than twelve.

Damned shame.

He holstered his gun, mounted his horse, and rode out of Kendall, Texas.

His job was done, and there had been some unfortunate incidentals, but that's all they were.

Incidentals.

II

Santee, New Mexico

When Decker rode into Santee he was not a happy man. He was leading a horse with a man slung over the saddle. The man had a nice price on his head, but Decker was supposed to have caught three men, each with a price on his head.

He rode right up to the sheriff's office and recognized the horse tethered outside. He dismounted and looked around, but the other two horses he had expected to see were nowhere in sight. The two wanted men were probably over at the undertaker's. He knew they weren't in jail, because they were dead.

He'd killed them.

He mounted the boardwalk and entered the sheriff's office without knocking. He didn't know the sheriff of this county, but that didn't matter.

As he entered, he saw a man sitting next

to the sheriff's desk. The man turned in his chair and his eyes widened in recognition.

"Wellman," the bounty hunter said coldly, ignoring the sheriff completely.

The lawman frowned and stood up.

"Who are you? What do you mean busting into my —"

"My name is Decker."

"Oh," the sheriff said, recognizing the name. "Ain't this my lucky day. Two bounty hunters in one day. Who have you got?"

"I've got Ross Parmenter outside."

"Dead, of course."

"Do you know any other way Parmenter would have come in?" Decker asked.

"No," the lawman admitted. "This feller just put in for Parmenter's sidekicks. He's got a two-thousand-dollar chit. I guess the five-thousand-dollar chit goes to you."

"Wrong," Decker said.

"What?" the sheriff asked, puzzled.

"I get the whole bundle."

"I don't understand —"

"This man does," Decker said, moving closer to Wellman, who stood up hastily.

"Take it easy, Decker."

"Well then, fill me in," the sheriff said. He was an older man, in his early fifties, and had probably been the sheriff here for a good many years. "I want to know what's

13

going on."

"I'll tell you what's going on," Decker said. "He stole my meat."

"What?"

"He's crazy," Wellman said.

"I caught up to Parmenter's sidekicks before I caught up to him. They made their choice and I killed them. Then I hung them up so they'd still be there when I got back with Parmenter," Decker explained.

"You . . . hung them up?"

"I tied a rope around their ankles and hung them from a tree to keep the critters from getting at them. When I got back with Parmenter, they'd been cut down. I didn't know by who until just now." He knew Wellman, and he knew his horse, so he knew who he'd be facing when he entered the sheriff's office.

Wellman was a hard man, but only when he had things going his way.

That wasn't the case here.

"He stole my meat, and he's trying to steal my money."

"Meat?" the sheriff said. "Is that what those men are to you?"

"It's what they are now," Decker said. "You sign my chit for five thousand, Sheriff. The rest I'll get from Wellman, here."

"Not in my office —"

"You want me to take him to court for it?" Decker asked. "Or are you telling me I'm not entitled to that money?"

The sheriff wiped his mouth nervously, withering beneath Decker's hard gaze.

"I ain't saying that at all —"

"Then sign my chit."

Defeated, the sheriff sat down and started writing.

"Let's have it, Wellman."

"What? You're crazy, Decker —"

"On the desk."

"Wha—"

Decker closed his eyes just for a second, displaying tolerance for the last time.

"Put the chit on the desk, Wellman," he said, enunciating each word very carefully. Nervously, Wellman looked at the sawed-off, cut-down shotgun Decker wore in a specially constructed holster.

"Decker, we can split —" Wellman started, but the look in Decker's eyes caused him to hurriedly pull the chit from his shirt pocket and put it on the desk, his hands shaking. That done, he stepped away from the desk and moved his hands away from his sides to show that they were empty.

"All right, all right," he said, backing away from the desk. "Jesus, Decker, they were just hanging there, swinging in the breeze.

15

How was I to know they were yours?"

"You know *me*, Wellman," Decker said, picking up the chits. "If I ever catch you stealing from me again . . ." he began, but thought better of threatening the man in front of a witness — especially a lawman.

"Get out of here," he said, his voice low and threatening.

Wellman rushed from the office, slamming the door behind him.

"Your chit for Parmenter," the sheriff said, handing it to Decker.

"I'll take him over to the undertaker."

"What did you mean, he knows you?" the sheriff asked.

"Nobody else hangs their meat up the way I do, Sheriff," Decker explained. "Wellman's in the business. He knows my trademarks."

"Like the hangman's noose you always carry with you?"

Decker stared at the sheriff, who apparently knew that trademark pretty well.

"Yes, like the hangman's noose. Have you got any new paper in, Sheriff?"

"Don't let any grass grow under your feet, do you?" the lawman said. "Well, as a matter of fact, I got some paper in on the Baron."

"On the Baron?" Decker said, surprised. "He's a killer, but he's usually careful

16

enough to avoid drawing paper."

"Well, not this time," the sheriff said. "He gunned down a kid, a twelve-year-old boy."

"What? He'd never take a job like that. Not on a boy."

"You know him?"

"I know his rep."

"Well, he killed a man named Carver and two others. One of them was probably the target. The kid came along later, and the Baron gunned him down."

"It must have been an accident."

"That mean you don't want any part of the reward?"

Decker looked at the figure on the poster the sheriff handed him. Ten thousand dollars.

"Or do you just not want any part of the Baron?" the sheriff asked. "Be an interesting matchup, you gotta admit."

"Thanks for the chits, Sheriff. I'll go over to the bank after I drop Parmenter off."

He left the sheriff's office, still holding on to the Baron's poster. After he took care of the body, and his horse, Decker entered the saloon. He ordered a beer, took it to a table, then unfolded the poster and stared at the picture of the Baron.

The Baron had been plying his trade as a hired killer for more than seven years without ever having made a mistake that Decker knew of. He guessed that the old saying was never more true.

There's always a first time.

CHAPTER ONE

Under normal circumstances, Decker's first move when he started hunting someone was to go to the place his quarry had last been seen. In this case, that would be Kendall, Wyoming.

This, however, was not a normal circumstance.

This time Decker was chasing another professional — not that bank robbery or train robbery weren't professions, but there was something about bounty hunting and hiring out as a killer that made them more closely related.

They were both man hunters. The only difference was that when the killer found his man, his job wasn't over until he killed him. At least the bounty hunter had the option of bringing his man in alive.

No, now that Decker was hunting a pro, there was no need to go to Kendall, Wyoming. There would be nothing there to help him. What he had to do was talk to another pro, another professional killer.

And he knew just the man — Joe Rigger.

There was only one problem with that. Joe Rigger had sworn that the next time he saw Decker, he'd kill him.

That was just something that Decker would have to deal with the best he could.

Finding Joe Rigger would be no problem. He always stayed in the same town between jobs. His profession had once been the same as Decker's, but five years ago he had switched from hunter to killer. Decker had always felt that Rigger changed professions because, with Decker around, he could no longer claim to be the best bounty hunter in the business.

Until the arrival of the Baron he *had* been the best professional killer around. Now his status was open to debate — to everyone but Rigger.

That was what Decker was counting on to get Rigger to help him.

Rigger was a Texan, and although it wasn't general knowledge, Decker knew that between jobs he stayed in the town of El Segundo, right across the border from Mexico. It was the perfect place; in case the law ever came looking for him, the border would be readily accessible. Of course, before the law came looking for him they'd need some kind of proof that he had killed in cold blood. Rigger was too good, too careful to ever leave anything like that behind him. Even if he couldn't get his target to face him fairly, he killed him anyway — and managed to be able to claim to be somewhere else at the time of the killing.

Everyone knew that Joe Rigger was a killer, but no one could ever prove it.

Except Decker. He'd been an eyewitness to one of Rigger's murders, but since the target had been a man Decker was hunting, and since Rigger had walked away from the body, Decker had been able to turn the corpse in for the bounty. That was the reason Rigger had sworn to kill him, for collecting a bounty on a man he had killed. He claimed it wasn't fair, or right, but Decker couldn't see the sense of letting the corpse rot without someone collecting the reward.

That had been a few years ago, just before the Baron had appeared on the scene. Decker wondered if Rigger was still angry.

He'd find out soon enough.

Decker entered El Segundo under the cover of night. He didn't want to run into Rigger by accident. He had a definite idea about

21

how to handle their first face-to-face meeting in three years.

He knew that Rigger owned the Hunter Saloon and kept the entire second floor for his own use. If anyone wanted to dally with one of Rigger's girls after hours, he'd have to supply the hotel room.

Decker walked his gelding, John Henry, behind the saloon and left him there. He moved around to the front of the saloon again and peeked through the window to make sure Rigger wasn't there. If he had been, Decker would have made his entry through the second floor. Since Rigger wasn't inside, that meant he was already upstairs.

Unless he was away on a job. If that was the case, Decker knew he'd have to find another angle to work.

He entered the saloon and walked to the bar. The place was about half full. It wasn't the biggest saloon in town, and Decker wondered how much business it usually did. Of course, Rigger's livelihood didn't depend on it, so half full was probably fine with him.

Decker ordered a beer from the bartender, a heavyset man with hands like hams and the face of a pig.

Beer in hand, he turned his back to the bar and checked the room. There were two girls working it, a fairly attractive blonde who had seen better days and a young brunette with the face of a schoolteacher and the body of a — well, no schoolteacher Decker had ever known had had a body like that.

The blonde was sitting on a man's lap, and the brunette, who had just dropped off some drinks at another table, was returning to the bar.

He didn't see anyone else working the saloon, so he assumed that either the bartender or one of the girls would know where Rigger was.

Looking closely at the younger girl, he decided she was his best bet. She'd be most likely to give Rigger's whereabouts away without meaning to.

As she approached the bar he touched her arm lightly.

"Two beers, Carl," she said to the bartender, then she turned her eyes — violet eyes, he noticed — toward Decker and went to work. "Can I help you?" she asked flirtatiously.

"Sure can," he said and smiled. She smiled back, a slow, sexy smile that would come easier and better after some more practice.

"You gonna tell me how?" she asked.

"Where's Rigger?"

Her smile slipped and for an instant — just for a split second — she glanced up at the ceiling.

"Who?" she asked innocently, but her eyes had said, "He's upstairs."

"Joe Rigger, the fella who owns this place."

The bartender returned with the beers the girl had ordered. He leaned across the bar and said, "Trouble, Viola?"

"This man is looking for someone named Rigger," Viola said. "He says he owns this saloon."

"I own this place, friend," the bartender said. "Can I help you?"

"No," Decker said, "you can't."

"There's no Rigger here."

"Fine, if you say so."

"I say so," the man said.

As the big man's right shoulder dipped, Decker pulled out his gun and laid it across the bar so that no one in the room could see it but the bartender and Viola.

"Put the shotgun on the bar, slowly," Decker said, his low voice menacing. Clutching the tray of beer, Viola started to move away but Decker said, "Uh-uh, sweetheart. Stay right there."

She stiffened, then stood still.

"On the bar, Carl. Easy, so we don't start

24

any trouble."

"You're the one looking for trouble, mister."

"No, I'm looking for Joe Rigger. I'm a friend of his."

"Sure . . ." the bartender said, gingerly lifting his shotgun up onto the bar.

"Break it and unload it."

The bartender opened the shotgun and slid the shells out, holding them in one hand.

"Put the shells in my shirt pocket."

The bartender did so, jamming them in forcefully. Decker let the man have his little moment of triumph.

"What makes you think I don't have more shells back here?" the bartender asked.

"Oh, I know you do. But by the time you can get them loaded, you'll be dead. Now, look into my eyes and tell me I'm lying."

The bartender tried to match Decker's stare but finally looked away.

"Yeah, you know I'm not lying," Decker said. "Now, both of you stay right where you are until I'm upstairs."

"You can't —" the bartender started, but he stopped when Decker cocked his gun.

"You do what I tell you, bartender, you hear?"

"I hear."

Decker eased the hammer back down and slid the gun into his holster.

"You understand, darlin'?" he asked the girl.

"Yes," she murmured. "I understand."

"You're gonna get yourself killed, my friend," the bartender said.

"Well now, that's my problem, isn't it?"

"You bet," the bartender said. "You bet it is. Go on up, go ahead. You won't ever come down again."

Decker smiled and said, "You wish."

Backing away from the bar, he moved toward the stairs. He didn't turn until he felt them behind him. Even then he kept an eye on the bartender over his shoulder. If the man went for his gun, he'd have to do something. Maybe he should have taken the shotgun with him, he thought, but he didn't expect the bartender had the guts to make the move.

He was right.

Upstairs he saw that there had once been several doors in the hallways, but all except one had been boarded up. The upstairs had probably been converted to one big apartment for Rigger.

He went to the single door and kicked it in.

Rigger sat straight up on his bed and

lunged for the gun on the headboard. At the same time he pushed the woman who was with him off of him. She fell to the floor, naked, in a tangle of bedsheets.

"Don't!" Decker snapped. "Don't do it, Joe."

Rigger frowned for a moment, then said, "Decker!" in disbelief.

"Hello, Joe," Decker said. "Jeez, you look like shit."

CHAPTER TWO

"Put the gun up, Deck," Joe Rigger said. "What's the big idea?"

"Don't tell me that you've forgotten your promise of three years ago."

"Promise?" Rigger said, frowning. He was still upright in bed, stark naked, and the woman on the floor was gathering all the bedclothes around her — but not quickly enough to keep Decker from seeing all she had to show.

"I haven't forgotten," Decker stated simply.

Rigger thought a moment, then said, "Oh, that!" and smiled for the first time. "You don't mean to say that you think I'm still angry over that. Come on, Deck. Put up the gun and we'll have a drink and talk about old times."

"Not until I have your gun, Joe."

Rigger frowned. "You're serious?" he asked.

"Dead serious."

Rigger, whose face always held a deceptively placid look, even just before he killed, shrugged and said, "Well, all right, then."

He started to reach for the gun and Decker said, "Not you, Joe! The woman."

Rigger looked at Decker and said, "What is it, Deck? I know you're not afraid of me."

"I have a healthy respect for you, Joe. I always have. I know what you can do with a gun."

Rigger withdrew his hand and said, "All right. Felicia, give the man my gun."

The woman on the floor — a busty brunette in her late twenties — said, "Joe, I ain't got any clothes on."

"Come on now, Felicia, don't be shy," Joe Rigger said. "Decker's an old friend of mine."

"A friend?" she said in disbelief.

"Sure, from way back. Besides, it's not like he didn't already see all there is to see. Come on, sweet. Give the man my gun."

The girl stared at Rigger, then at Decker, then shrugged and stood up, dropping the bedclothes. Her breasts were full and her nipples dark. Her slim waist contrasted with her rounded hips. She moved slowly, almost seductively, around the bed, as if enjoying the fact that both men's eyes were on her.

Or was that what Rigger had in mind?

As she started to slide the gun from the holster Decker said, "Bring the whole thing."

Obeying, she slid the holster from the bedpost and turned to him with it. Had he allowed her to approach him, with his eyes firmly fixed on her body, Rigger could easily have leaped from the bed onto him.

"Put it on that table over there," Decker ordered, pointing away from himself.

She paused, then nodded and obeyed, walking away from him, but not so far that he couldn't keep his eyes on both her and Rigger.

"Now you can leave," Decker told her.

She looked at Rigger, who nodded and said, "Go ahead, Felicia."

"Like this?" she demanded, horrified at the prospect.

Decker allowed her to dress, and then she moved quickly to the door.

"Do you want her to bring reinforcements, Joe?" Decker asked as she paused with her hand on the knob.

"Yes," Rigger said, then smiled and added, "a bottle of whiskey and two glasses." He looked directly at the woman and said, "And that's all, Felicia."

She nodded and left.

"Can I get dressed now?" Rigger asked.

"Sure, Joe," Decker said, holstering his gun.

Rigger stood up and dressed, except for his boots.

"We can go into the next room. It's my . . . office."

"Lead the way."

"I've got some guns in there, but I don't intend to go for any of 'em. As far as I'm concerned," he said, leading the way, "this is a visit between two friends."

"You've got a funny way of remembering things, Joe."

In Rigger's office there was a desk with two chairs — one behind, one in front — and a divan against one wall. Rigger sat behind his desk, and Decker took the chair in front.

"If this is not a friendly visit, Decker, then why *are* you here? It's not really that old threat, is it?"

"Threats to kill a man don't die of old age, Joe."

"Well, this one did. Only it died a young death, Decker. I decided not long after our last meeting that it was stupid of me to have threatened you."

"I never got word of that."

Rigger laughed.

"I never thought you took me seriously."

"I always take you seriously, Joe."

There was a knock on the office door. Viola stood there uncertainly, carrying a tray with a bottle of whiskey and two glasses.

"Viola, come on in," Rigger said. "Meet my friend, Decker."

"We met downstairs," Decker said.

"You did? Did you also meet Carl?"

"The bartender? Yes," Decker said. He took the shotgun shells out of his shirt pocket and dropped them on the tray Viola was holding. "These are his."

Viola put the tray down, removed the bottle and glasses, and then picked it up again. She stared pointedly at the shotgun shells.

"Take them down to Carl, Viola," Rigger said. "Tell him if it had been any man other than Decker, he'd be fired right now."

The young woman nodded.

"And don't leave after closing," Rigger called after her as she left. "I may want you."

"All right."

As she left, Decker smiled and looked at Rigger.

"What about Felicia?"

"Felicia? Oh, you mean wanting Viola? I don't want her for me, Deck, I want her for you."

"Oh."

"Unless you'd prefer Felicia?"

"If it comes to a choice, I'll make it."

"Meanwhile," Rigger said, grabbing the bottle and pouring two drinks, "have a drink and tell me what brings you here."

Decker accepted the glass and said, "The Baron."

Rigger barely let his feelings show on his face as he heard the name.

"What about him?" he asked, all bantering tone gone from his voice.

"I'm hunting him."

"The Baron?" Rigger asked in surprise. "What's he done to deserve you on his trail?"

"What he's always done," Decker said. "Same thing you do."

"Then why aren't you after me?"

"There's no price on your head."

"And there is on his?"

"Yep."

"How much?"

Decker paused, wondering if the size of the price might drive Rigger back into the bounty-hunting trade.

"Fifteen thousand."

Rigger whistled.

"Who'd he kill to earn that amount?"

"A boy," Decker said. "A child."

"A child?" Rigger said. "He hired out to kill a child?"

"He killed the kid after he'd killed his quarry."

"By accident?"

Decker shrugged.

"No, that's right. You wouldn't care, would you? Not as long as that fifteen thousand dollars is on his head."

"High talk from a former bounty hunter turned killer."

"Touché," Rigger said, raising his glass. "So, if you're on his trail, why look me up?"

"Because he's a professional. Normal methods will not work with him."

"So you want me to help you?"

"Yes."

"How? I don't know where he is."

"You're a killer."

"I don't deny that."

"And so is he. You can give me some idea of how he thinks, of where he'd be."

"If he's smart, he's holed up somewhere."

"Where?"

"I don't know where."

"Find out."

"How can I find out?"

"I knew where you were. Somebody must know where he is. How do people get in touch with you when they want you?"

Rigger rubbed his jaw. Decker knew that there was a man you got in touch with when you wanted to hire Joe Rigger, and that man was in San Francisco. There had to be a man you contacted when you wanted the Baron.

Rigger could find out who that man was.

"You must think a lot of me," Rigger stated.

"Not a whole lot," Decker said, and Rigger laughed.

"You're gonna have to give me time to think this over. After all, I've got to have some loyalty to my profession."

Decker thought about Wellman and how much loyalty he had to his profession, and he knew that Rigger was talking through his hat. Still, Rigger would need time to figure out his angle, how he could benefit from helping Decker.

"All right," Decker said. "Sleep on it, then." He drained his glass and put it on the desk. "I'll be at the hotel."

"You can stay here —"

Decker interrupted Rigger by rising.

"I'll stay at the hotel, Joe."

Rigger shrugged and said, "Suit yourself. I'll let you know what I decide in the morning."

Decker turned and headed for the door.

"Hey, Deck."

"Yeah?"

"If you were to choose between Felicia and Viola, which would it be?"

Decker thought for only a second and said, "Viola."

Rigger nodded and said, "Good choice."

CHAPTER THREE

Decker had to awaken the liveryman to get his horse taken care of, and then he had to rouse the desk clerk at the hotel in order to get a room. He had just removed his boots and shirt when there was a knock at his door. He answered it, his gun in hand.

It was Viola. Her dark hair fell loosely about her pale shoulders, and she had changed into a dress with a very revealing neckline. He had a tantalizing view of the creamy cleft between her breasts.

"What are you doing here?"

"Well, what kind of way is that to greet a lady?" she asked.

"I wasn't expecting you. As a matter of fact, I wasn't expecting anyone."

"I'm sorry to disappoint you."

"Oh, I'm not disappointed."

"Then can I come in?"

"I, uh — what for?" Decker asked.

"Rigger told me . . . that you chose me,"

she said, looking puzzled. "Isn't that true?"

"Well, it . . . it's true and it's not," Decker said, annoyed that he was stammering. He was not exactly a ladies' man, although he knew what to do with a lady when he wanted her.

"I'm confused."

"Don't be," Decker said, "and don't be offended, but I'm really not looking for any company tonight."

"Oh, I see," she said. "You tell a lady to get lost but you don't want her to be offended."

"There's no reason for you to be offended," Decker said. "You're very lovely, but —"

"Don't you like girls?"

"I like girls just fine," Decker snapped. "I just don't want to take anything from Joe Rigger right now."

She frowned. "I thought you were friends."

"Not exactly."

"Now I am confused," she said, "but not offended."

"That's good."

"How long will you be in town?"

"Probably not very long."

"Oh," she said. "That's a pity. Well, good night, then."

"Good night."

After she had gone he sat on the bed and wondered if he hadn't made a mistake sending her away, then decided that he hadn't, and went to sleep.

He had a dream, and in the dream he was twenty-one and was accused of killing a woman.

He had been hired by the woman's husband to do odd jobs around their ranch. The woman was older than he by about ten years, but she was a very handsome female. Although it wasn't easy, Decker had managed to decline her advances.

Unfortunately, she did not take his rejection kindly and told her husband he tried to rape her. Decker and the man had a huge fight, during which Decker knocked the man down in front of his wife. Doubly embarrassed, the man fired Decker and never paid him the money he owed him for the work he'd already done. That was fine with Decker, though. He just wanted to get away from both of them.

He dreamt he was leaving town on foot when the posse rode up and arrested him for raping and killing her.

The husband had told them that Decker did it. Then in his dream Decker saw himself in court, where a judge eagerly convicted him.

The sheriff of the town believed Decker to be innocent, but Decker was convicted and sentenced to hang.

In the dream Decker could feel the noose around his neck, and he could smell his own fear . . .

Suddenly he awoke, still smelling that old fear. He rose and went to the pitcher and basin on the dresser and washed away the stench of his fear.

He remembered what had happened while he was waiting for the trapdoor to be sprung from beneath him.

He had actually gotten as far as the gallows, and the hangman had put the noose over his neck. Decker had given himself up for dead, had known that within seconds he would be executed for a crime he'd never committed. It had only been at the last moment that Mike Farrell, the sheriff, brought the real killer in and made him confess.

The killer was the husband.

Decker was not the first one that the woman had thrown herself at. That, combined with the fact that Decker had knocked him down, made the man angry enough to attack his own wife. In his fury he had killed her by accident, then, frightened, he had blamed Decker.

Nobody apologized. In fact, when Decker

had walked down from the gallows nobody was even there anymore. They'd gone home disappointed that they weren't going to see a hanging.

Sheriff Mike Farrell resigned and left town after that, and Decker rode with him for a short time. Farrell tried to get Decker to take up being a lawman, but Decker had other ideas.

He became a bounty hunter. His reasoning was that he wanted to be able to get to the ones who were going to be hanged and satisfy himself that they were guilty before he handed them over to the law. He didn't want what happened to him to happen to any other innocent man — ever.

The noose that he carried was a reminder of what had almost happened to him and why he took up bounty hunting. Every once in a while he lost sight of his reason, but the noose never failed to bring it back to him.

He dried his face and chest, wiping the towel under his arms, where the smell of fear persisted.

He returned to the bed then, wishing he had a bottle of whiskey in the room with him.

Actually, he was wishing he had Viola in the room with him. She would have kept him from thinking of his past, and might have kept him from dreaming about it.

The knock on the door in the morning woke him. As he opened his eyes he couldn't even remember falling asleep. Cautiously he opened the door to find Viola standing in the hall.

"Good morning," he said.

She sniffed and said, "You smell terrible."

"I had a bad night," he muttered. "To what do I owe the pleasure of this return engagement?"

"Don't flatter yourself. Joe sent me over to invite you to breakfast."

"When and where?"

"His room, half an hour."

"Tell him I'll be there."

"Do everybody a favor," she said.

"What?"

"Take a bath first."

CHAPTER FOUR

When Decker reached the saloon he found the front door open. They weren't open for business, but the bartender was inside, just starting to take the chairs down off the tables.

"What can I do for you?" he asked Decker coldly.

"I got an invitation from Rigger for breakfast."

"Oh yeah," the bartender said. "He's waiting for you upstairs. Tell him I'll send breakfast up."

"I'll tell him."

Decker went up the stairs and knocked on the door of Rigger's room. It was opened by Viola.

"Well," she said, putting her hand on her hip, "don't we smell pretty."

Decker stepped past her into the room.

"Decker, glad you could come! Viola, go down and tell Carl —"

"Carl said he'd send breakfast up."

"Great." Rigger looked at the girl and said, "Okay, get lost."

"Sure you don't want me to stay?"

"I'm sure."

Viola looked at Decker, then turned and left.

"That any way to treat a lady?" Decker asked.

Rigger laughed.

"If she were a lady, she sure wouldn't be working here," he said. "Besides, she loves it when I treat her like that. She thinks it means I love her."

"Do you love her?"

"I love all my girls," Rigger said, spreading his arms magnanimously. "Come on, Decker. Let's go inside and have a seat. Breakfast'll be here soon."

Rigger led Decker into another room, where a large, round table was set up with everything you'd need for breakfast — except breakfast.

"Have a seat. You're gonna love the food. Carl does things with eggs nobody else can."

"I'm sure. Could we get to the discussion at hand?"

"Hmm? Oh, you mean what we talked about last night."

"Right. The Baron."

Rigger scratched underneath his chin and looked like he was concentrating on something.

"Yeah, I guess I could give you some idea of where to look. I can't say he's there, mind you, but you could start looking."

"Where?"

"Up north. Montana."

"Montana? Why would he be holed up in Montana?"

Rigger shrugged and said, "He likes the cold. Is it cold in Russia?"

"I don't know," Decker said.

"Well, the way I hear it, when he's between jobs he goes up Montana way."

"Where? Does he have a spread up there?"

Rigger shrugged and said, "Beats me. I guess you'll have to go up there and find out."

"I guess I'll have to."

"Montana's a big place."

"It's a place to start."

Decker stood up just as the door opened and Carl entered with breakfast.

"You ain't leaving before you eat, are you?" Rigger asked.

That had been Decker's intention, but suddenly he was hungry. Must have had something to do with the smell of bacon and eggs and biscuits and fried potatoes.

"After Carl went to all this trouble?" he asked. "Hell no."

"Good!" Rigger said. "Set it right down, Carl. You got a couple of hungry hombres here."

Over breakfast they talked about anything but the Baron. Rigger spoke about El Segundo and why he liked it there.

"It's peaceful," he said. "I make my living with my gun, Deck, but I'm pretty sure I ain't gonna have to use it here."

"Isn't it a little dangerous?" Decker asked.

"What?"

"Having one place where you stay between jobs. You here in Texas, the Baron in Montana."

Rigger shrugged.

"Not many people know where to find me," he said.

"I knew."

"You're in the business."

"Not your business."

"Well, then, you know me. You don't know the Baron, that's why you had to come to me."

"It still sounds dangerous, always returning to the same place."

"Everybody's got to have a place to stay, Decker," Rigger said. "A place to relax, let

46

down their guard." Rigger leaned forward and said, "Don't you have a place, Decker?"

Decker stood up and shook his head.

"I never let my guard down, Joe. Thanks for the breakfast, and the information."

"I'm glad we got our old . . . argument cleared up, Deck. I'd like to think of you as a friend."

"Why's that?"

Rigger smiled and said, "I never kill friends."

"I guess I should find that encouraging. Give Carl my compliments."

"I'm almost tempted to come along with you," Rigger said to Decker's retreating back.

"Why don't you?"

Rigger thought a moment, then shook his head.

"It wouldn't do. Word might get out that I went after the Baron because of —"

"Jealousy?" Decker asked.

Rigger shrugged.

As Decker turned to walk to the door, Rigger called out, "Hey, Deck!"

"Yeah?" Decker said, turning with his hand on the doorknob.

"Um, anything I tell you stays between you and me, right?"

"Sure."

"I mean, I wouldn't want it to get around that I told you where the Baron was."

"You don't have anything to worry about. Besides, when you get right down to it, you really haven't told me where he is, have you?"

Rigger smiled. "Try a town in Wyoming called Douglas, near the North Platte River. Look for a man named Calder."

"Calder? Who's he?"

"He's the man you go to see when you want to hire the Baron."

Surprised at the information — and that Rigger would be willing to give it — Decker gave the other man a small salute and left the room.

Downstairs Decker didn't see Carl, but he did see the girl, Viola. She was dressed for work, even though it was early. She wore a silver dress with a deep, plunging neckline and probably thought she looked sexy as all hell. Decker still thought she was a little too innocent-looking for this line of work.

"Are you and Joe finished?" she asked.

"All done," Decker said. "He's all yours."

"Not yet," she said, cocking one hip, "but he will be."

"Good luck, honey — you'll need it."

Joe Rigger didn't love anybody but Joe

Rigger. Viola was going to have to learn that the hard way.

CHAPTER FIVE

Douglas was a fair-sized town about forty miles east of the larger town of Casper, Wyoming, and about eighty miles west of the Nebraska border. It was almost three hundred miles south of Montana. It had everything a town should have if you were going to use it for a base: a hotel and a telegraph office.

Decker put his horse up in the livery and then carried his rifle and saddlebags to the hotel.

"Will you be staying long, sir?" the clerk asked him. He was a dapper man with slicked-down hair, and he smelled of cheap cologne.

"That depends," Decker said, signing the register.

"On what, sir?"

"On how long it takes me to find a man named Calder."

"Who, sir?"

"Calder," Decker said. He put the pen down and stared at the clerk. "You don't know anyone by that name?"

The clerk thought a moment, then shook his head and said, "No, sir. Does the gentleman have a first name?"

"I'm sure he does," Decker said. "Can I have my key, please?"

"Of course, sir," the man said. "Room 7. It overlooks the street."

"What does Room 8 overlook?"

"Just the alley."

"Is there a roof or ledge outside the window?"

"No, sir."

"I'll take that one."

"As you wish, sir."

The clerk replaced the key to number 7 and handed him the key to number 8.

"If there's anything else —"

"I'll let you know," Decker said. "Thanks."

He picked up his rifle and saddlebags and ascended the stairs to the second floor. Once in the room he dropped his gear on the bed and walked to the window. Sure enough, it overlooked an alley. Across from him was a blank wall. There was no way of telling what kind of building it belonged to. Its roof, however, extended another floor above his window. There was no access there. He was satisfied that the room was fairly secure from outside entry — except for the door. He fixed that by taking the one straight-backed wooden chair in the room and jamming it under the doorknob.

He had ridden all day and was tired, even more than he was hungry or thirsty. He took off his boots, reclined on the bed, and fell as deeply asleep as his instincts would let him. At the slightest sound, he'd be instantly awake and alert. Left alone, he'd be able to sleep for about an hour, then go in search of a drink and a meal.

The drink was a shot of whiskey at the saloon, followed by a beer.

"Maybe you can help me," Decker said to the bartender after he swallowed the last of the beer.

"I just did, friend," the man said. He was a sloppy fat man with huge forearms that looked as if they might once have held some muscle. Maybe there still was some beneath the surface. His face was a mass of bumps, dominated by a lumpy nose. He had either been a wrestler or a bare-knuckled boxer.

"I need to find a man."

"I supply drinks," the man said, "and you can probably find a woman in here. We don't deal in men."

"Look, friend —" Decker said, putting his hand on the bartender's arm. The bartender quickly closed his other hand around Decker's wrist and squeezed. Decker found out that the man still had plenty of muscle.

"You wanna ask me a question, you go ahead and ask, *friend,* but that don't entitle you to touch me." With that he took Decker's hand off his arm and then released him. "And it don't necessarily entitle you to an answer."

"I'm looking for a man named Calder," Decker said. Holding his hand below the bar level so the barkeep couldn't see, he began to flex it, trying to bring it back to life.

"So?"

"You heard of him?"

"What if I have?"

"I'd like to see him."

"And what if I haven't?"

"I'd still like to see him."

"What for?"

"That's between him and me."

"If I did know him, where would he be able to find you?"

"Right here, after about an hour."

"Where you gonna be for that hour?"

"Getting some dinner. Know a good place?"

"There's a café down the street. It ain't the best food in the country, but it'll do."

"Thanks. I'll be back here in an hour."

The bartender shrugged, as if he didn't care one way or the other.

Before going to the café Decker stopped in at the sheriff's office.

The man seated behind the desk looked up.

"Can I help you?" he asked.

"My name's Decker," the bounty hunter said, moving toward the desk. "Just wanted to check in with you. I just arrived in town."

The lawman stood, showing himself to be a tall man of medium build, not thin, not heavy.

"Why would you be checking in with me?"

"Isn't that what a stranger does when he comes to town?"

The man laughed, showing yellowed teeth.

"Not in my experience."

"Well, I'm a bounty hunter on the trail of a man."

The lawman frowned and said, "That's different. I'm obliged that you came here and introduced yourself." He stuck out his hand. "My name's Calder, Sheriff Sam Calder."

Decker paused only slightly before taking the man's hand and shaking it.

Finding Calder had been easier than he'd thought.

CHAPTER SIX

Over dinner, Decker considered his options.

He had left the sheriff's office without approaching the man about the Baron. For one thing, he didn't know if the lawman was the right Calder. For another, he'd already made contact at the saloon and was probably better off going through the proper channels. If the sheriff *was* the right Calder, let *him* approach Decker.

At the café Decker ordered a steak with potatoes and onions, some biscuits, and a pot of coffee. The bartender had been right. The food wasn't the best, but it was edible and better than the beef jerky and beans he'd been eating on the trail. As for the coffee, Decker rarely found better coffee than he prepared for himself over a fire.

After dinner he went back to the saloon and ordered a beer from the bartender. From the big man's demeanor, no one would have known that Decker had already been in the saloon once. Decker did not speak up. If that was the way the man wanted to play it, that was fine with him.

The saloon was fairly full now. Two private poker games were going on at opposite ends of the room and a couple of saloon girls were working the room, both looking more suited to their occupation than Viola had back in El Segundo. These women were older and knew how to work a crowd of men, not playing favorites but making each of the men feel special.

Decker took his beer over to one of the poker games to watch. Ten minutes later, when a chair opened up, he slid into it.

"You gents mind some new blood?"

"Not as long as you got some new money to go with it," one of them said, laughing at his own joke. The other three men at the table did not last. The joking man was apparently the big winner. He had a very red face, which Decker at first suspected came from laughing. He soon discovered that the man's face was naturally that color.

The deal fell to Decker and he dealt out a hand of five-card stud. He'd dealt himself a small straight, but the red-faced man was betting two pair like they were invincible. The other three men dropped out of the hand, and Decker decided to let the big winner have it. He didn't like it when a new man sat in on a game, drew the deal and immediately made a winning hand. Anybody losing would look at that suspiciously.

Two rounds later he drew a third king to a pair in a hand of draw poker and beat the red-faced man's three threes without tipping his hand.

"Looks like we've got us a player," the red-faced man said.

"Somebody ought to start beating you," one of the other players mumbled.

Fortune eventually turned for one of the other men, who started winning big. Decker, too, won a few hands and was ahead. Red Face started to lose and no longer had cause to laugh.

In fact, he was decidedly unhappy.

"Looks like your luck changed as soon as the stranger sat down," he said to the man who'd started winning.

"You're as much a stranger to me as he is," the man stated.

The other man obviously wasn't too sure about that, but as long as he kept his feelings to himself, Decker knew there'd be no trouble.

Over the next hour Decker won a little, the previous winner lost a lot, and the new winner was winning the most. The other players were holding their own.

This did not sit well with the red-faced man, who finally decided to speak out.

"I don't like the way this game is going," he said sullenly.

"You think we do?" one of the other losers said.

"I wonder why you started winning as soon as this man sat down?" Red Face said, indicating Decker.

"Beats me, but I'm sure glad he came along. Changed my luck for sure."

The man who spoke was watching Decker. Although he was winning, it was clear that Red Face was intimating that Decker was doing the cheating.

Decker looked at Red Face and said, "If you're not willing to lose your money, friend, I suggest you move on. Losing is part of this game."

"A *big* part," one of the other losers mumbled.

"I don't mind losing," Red Face said. "My luck just changed a little too quick to suit me, is all."

"Talk like that is not going to make your luck any better," Decker stated. "Just what is it you're accusing me of, friend?"

Red Face looked into Decker's eyes and suddenly seemed nervous. He realized he'd said too much and now seemed to want to back off.

"I'm not saying nothing."

"And you're not playing in this game anymore, either," Decker told him.

"I got money on the table," Red Face snapped.

"You're still a little ahead, friend," Decker said softly. "Why not quit now and save yourself . . . further embarrassment?"

Red Face looked at the other men at the table and, finding no support from any of them, picked up his money and stood.

He paused, as if he wanted to say something, but before he could Decker said, "Don't change your mind."

Red Face hesitated, then turned abruptly and walked out of the saloon. It was only then that Decker realized that Sheriff Calder had been watching.

"How long have you been here, Sheriff?" he asked as the lawman approached the table.

"Long enough," Calder said. "Can we talk?"

"Gentlemen," Decker said, surrendering his cards, "it's been interesting."

He rose and faced the sheriff.

"I like the way you handled that."

"I don't like being called a cheater."

60

"Most men would consider that grounds for killing."

"I never kill over a card game," Decker said. "It makes it hard to get players next time."

Calder laughed. "I like that, too."

"I'm glad you approve. Where do we go to talk?"

"There's an office in the back," the sheriff said, pointing.

"The owner lets you use it?"

Sheriff Calder grinned and said, "I am the owner."

CHAPTER SEVEN

Decker followed the sheriff to the back office, smiling at the fact that the town sheriff also owned the saloon. In most places, that was considered a conflict of interest, of sorts.

"Does the town council know about this?" Decker asked as they entered the office.

"Of course," Calder said. "I'm the head of the town council."

"I see."

Decker regarded the man for a few seconds. Sheriff Calder did not seem to be a particularly formidable man, physically. What was it, Decker wondered, that had apparently enabled the man to obtain the run of the town?

Could it be because he was the Baron's contact? Perhaps it was the Baron that the townspeople were afraid of. That seemed very likely to Decker. He knew of a man who once was able to terrify a town because his brother was a known gunman. When the brother was killed by someone faster, the town turned on the man and cast him out.

What would happen to Sheriff Calder, Decker wondered, once he brought the Baron in for the bounty?

It would be interesting to come back and find out.

"Have a seat," the sheriff said.

For now, however, Decker had to deal with Calder. He did as the other man instructed.

"Can I offer you a drink?"

"No, thanks."

"I understand you were in here earlier looking for me," Calder said, sitting behind his desk.

"I was looking for a man named Calder," Decker said. "At the time, I didn't know you were the sheriff."

"What about when you came to my office?"

"I didn't know your name, and then when you told me, I didn't know if you were the same Calder."

"I'm the only Calder in town," the lawman said. "If you didn't know who I was, why were you in here looking for me?"

Decker decided not to beat around the bush.

"I understand that if I want to hire the Baron I have to go through you."

The man did not answer right away, and when he did he didn't admit anything. Apparently he wasn't as willing to do away with beating around the bush as Decker was.

"The Baron? Should I know who that is?"

"I hope you do, or I made a trip for nothing."

"You just might have."

Decker leaned forward and said, "Let's not play games, Calder."

"Sheriff Calder," the lawman corrected him.

"You're proud of that star, aren't you?"

In answer, the sheriff looked at his badge and then wiped it with his sleeve.

"How long do you think you'd keep it without the Baron to back you up?"

"I don't need anybody to back me up."

"Then you do know the Baron."

"What do you want with him?"

"I want to hire him to do what he does best."

"What's that?"

"Kill."

Calder studied Decker intently for a few moments.

"You don't look like you need any help

doing that."

"I can't do this one," Decker said. "I need someone who's not . . . involved."

"Who do you want killed?"

"I'll tell that to the Baron."

"Can you afford him?"

"I don't know," Decker said. "What's he cost?"

Calder named a figure.

"I can cover that."

"I'd have to check you out, Decker."

"What's to check out? I told you who I am and what I do."

"How do I know you're not looking to cash in on the Baron?"

"Has he got a price on his head?" Decker asked innocently.

When Calder didn't answer, Decker said, "Even if he does, he can't very well solve my problem for me if I take him in for a bounty, can he?"

"You couldn't take him," the sheriff said.

"You may be right, but right now I'm more concerned with hiring him."

Again, Calder took some time before speaking.

"I'll have to get back to you."

"About what?"

"I'll have to find out if he's available."

"How long will that take?"

65

The man shrugged.

"A day, maybe two. Stick around town, play some poker. You'll hear from me."

That sounded to Decker like a dismissal, so he stood up.

"I'll need to see him within the next couple of weeks, Calder. I can't wait any longer than that."

"Like I said, give me a couple of days."

Decker nodded and went back into the saloon.

CHAPTER EIGHT

Back in his room, Decker heard the floor-boards creak outside his room. Instantly awake, he heard the noise again.

Silently he rolled off the bed, drawing his gun from the holster on the bedpost. Then he waited.

The floorboards creaked long enough to tell him that there was more than one person in the hall. He cocked the hammer on his gun and waited.

Suddenly, the door burst open, as if kicked, and there was a man in the doorway shooting at the bed. Decker could hear the bullets as they struck the mattress. Without even thinking he started firing himself.

The figure in the doorway staggered and then fell, and Decker saw another silhouette behind him. That man fired one quick shot into the room and then turned and ran down the hall.

Decker sprang to his feet, ran around the

bed, jumped over the body and burst into the hall. He could hear someone banging his way down the steps and ran after him, gun in hand. Luckily, he was cold when he went to bed and wore not only his long underwear, but his pants, as well. Unfortunately, he was barefoot and stubbed his toe just before he started down the steps. Ignoring the pain, he ran down the steps and into the lobby, where the startled desk clerk was staring at him.

"Which way did he go?" Decker demanded.

"What? What?"

He ran to the desk, grabbed the clerk's shirt, and pulled him halfway across the desk.

"Which way did he go, damn it?"

"Out the front door," the clerk said. Decker released him, and as he was going out the door he heard the man shouting, "What's happening, what's happening?"

Decker ran out into the street and looked both ways but didn't see anyone. He stood stock-still and simply listened. Since it was so late at night the saloons were closed and there was not any music or shouting. For this reason, he heard the sound of someone running to his right. He didn't so much hear the man running as he heard him breathing hard as he ran.

Decker moved to his right, not running but moving quickly. He was walking on the boardwalk, and since he was barefoot there was no possibility of his footsteps being heard. He was not running because he did not want to breathe heavily. Bare-chested, he was aware of a slight bite in the air.

Ahead of him he could hear the man's boots scraping and sliding alternately on dirt and the boardwalk. Decker quickened his pace, wanting to keep the man at least within earshot.

Finally Decker reached a point where he couldn't hear the man anymore. It was possible that he had stepped into a storefront along the way, but all of the doors seemed to be locked. Decker continued moving along, alert for any movement behind him, but when he came to an alley he felt certain that this was where the man went.

Decker flattened himself against the window and carefully peered around the corner. He listened intently for a few moments and thought he might have heard the sound of breathing — although it could have been his own.

Sliding into the alley, he wondered if it dead-ended or if he was wasting his time and the man was long gone. He moved cautiously, not staying to the center or to either side, but moving from side to side so as not to present an easy target.

He held his gun in his right hand, cradling the barrel with his left, all his senses alert. He was sweating, which was making his exposed flesh feel even colder than before.

As he went farther into the alley the darkness deepened but his night vision improved. Finally he could make out the end of the alley, which was indeed a dead end. There were some wooden cartons at the end, and he had to assume that the man was behind one of them.

"There are two ways out of here," Decker said aloud. "You can throw your gun out and we can walk out together, or I can walk out alone and leave you behind — dead."

He waited, and there was no response.

"The choice is yours," he added.

Two things tipped him off. He heard a sharp intake of breath and the sound of a boot sliding on the ground, and then the man moved quickly out from behind a carton, gun in hand. Decker squeezed the trigger and his shot caught the man in the stomach, punching it out through his back.

He knew it was useless to hope that the man was alive to question, so he turned to go back to the hotel before he caught pneumonia.

As he rushed through the lobby the clerk again shouted, "What's happening?" And then he called out, "Should I send for the sheriff?"

Decker didn't reply. He thought the sheriff already knew all about this.

Decker returned to his room and turned up the lamp. In the bright yellow light he leaned over and turned the man over. His bullet had traveled true, striking the man in the chest just where his heart was. He was dead and wouldn't be telling Decker anything.

He knew someone who would, however.

Decker, fully dressed and carrying his saddlebags and rifle, burst into the sheriff's office, startling the man behind the desk.

"What the —" Calder said, but before he could say any more Decker had dropped his saddlebags and was pointing his rifle at the lawman.

"Where do I find the Baron?" he demanded.

"What the hell are you doing, Decker? You're pointing a gun at a duly appointed —"

"Don't give me that shit, Calder," Decker

said. He moved closer so he could put the barrel of his rifle right beneath Calder's chin. The man tried to back away, but his chair hit the wall behind him and he couldn't go any farther.

"Your boys missed me, Calder, and I'm not about to give you a second chance."

"I don't know what —" Calder started to protest, but Decker pushed the barrel of the rifle right up against the man's Adam's apple, cutting him off.

"I'm going to ask you one more time," Decker said. "Where do I find the Baron?"

"He'll kill me —"

"I'll kill you, Calder, and I'm here right now."

"You can't do this to a lawman —"

"When I find the Baron and bring him in you won't be a lawman anymore, so I'm not worried about you."

"You should worry about the Baron, Decker," the sheriff said. "He'll kill you."

"I'll worry about that, Calder. Just tell me where he is."

"I'll — I'll —"

"Tell me!"

"All right, all right," Calder said. "I'll tell you where he is, because I know when you find him, he'll kill you."

"We'll see."

"Try up around the Powder River. I hear the Baron favors that area."

"What do you mean, you hear? How do you get in touch with him?"

"I don't," Calder said. "He gets in touch with me."

"When will you hear from him next?"

Calder shrugged and said, "When he's looking for more work."

"You don't know how to get in touch with him?"

Calder shook his head, his eyes fixed on the barrel of the rifle beneath his chin.

"If you're sending me to the Powder River for nothing, Calder, I'll be back."

"You won't be back, Decker."

"You better hope I'm not."

Decker removed the barrel from beneath the man's chin, reversed the rifle and slammed it into Calder's jaw. He needed the man to be out just long enough for him to saddle his horse and get out of town.

He picked up his saddlebags and left the office. Minutes later he was astride John Henry and riding out of town toward the Powder River.

CHAPTER NINE

Decker's trek to the Powder River area of Montana was long and uneventful. As he crossed the border into Montana from Wyoming it seemed to get noticeably colder. He pulled out his coat and put it on, turning up the fur collar.

The Powder River was born in Wyoming, ran about 140 miles north and then entered Montana, continuing for about 120 miles, give or take a mile or two for a bend here and there. That meant that Decker had 120 miles of river to follow, detouring for towns that were within easy reach — say a day's ride, at most.

Decker didn't think he'd have to ride to the end of the river. He was sure the Baron would probably rather be closer to the Wyoming border than deep in Montana. It would make it easier for him to get to Calder if he had to.

As he rode along the Powder River, the

first place he came to was more a settlement than a town. A sign just outside announced its name as BRENNER'S CROSSING.

There were more tents than buildings, although in several places there were some skeleton structures, one of which looked suspiciously like a church.

One of the tents had a handwritten wooden sign over the doorway that said saloon. He dismounted, let John Henry's reins fall to the ground, and entered the tent.

Inside, a bar had been fashioned out of several ten-foot-long wooden planks that had been stacked on barrels. There were a few men in the place sitting at makeshift tables. They looked like lumberjacks. One of them, a large, bearded fellow, stood out from the rest and seemed to be the center of attention at his table of five men.

Decker walked to the bar and asked, "Have you got cold beer?"

"As cold as you'll get around here."

"I'll take a chance."

The beer turned out to be lukewarm. He sipped at it, thinking about the Baron. Decker doubted that this would be the sort of place he'd hide out in. Most men needed women, and the Baron wasn't likely to find many around here — unless one of these tents was a whore house.

He finished his beer and called the bartender back.

"Any chance of getting some companionship around here?"

"You talking about women?" the man asked. A short man with a round belly and bad teeth, he didn't look like the type of man who knew a lot about where to find a woman.

"I'm talking about women."

"Not around here. You'd have to wait for Lilly's wagon to come through."

"Lilly's wagon?"

"Yep. Lilly's got herself a whore house on wheels. She makes the rounds of some of the lumber camps."

"I see. Any real towns hereabouts?"

"Most of them are like this, half town, half camp. We're hoping to build us a church and a saloon pretty soon so's we can be a real town."

"Well, if you're going to be a real town, those are the two buildings you'll need."

"You bet. Another beer?"

Decker made a face, then figured lukewarm beer was better than no beer.

"Yeah, give me another one."

When the bartender returned he said,

"You planning on staying?"

"I don't know. You got anything like a hotel?"

"There's a tent down at the end of the street that rents cots."

Sleeping in a tent on a cot wouldn't be much better than sleeping on the trail, Decker thought. As a matter of fact, sleeping on the trail would be better because he'd be able to build a fire and lie next to it.

"I guess I'll make camp somewhere."

"Don't get too far from the settlement," the bartender advised.

"Why?"

"Wolves."

"More than one?"

The man nodded.

"Got us a pack that's roaming around."

"They wouldn't get near a fire."

"Maybe not," the bartender said, "but you gotta think about your horse, too."

Decker knew he wouldn't have to worry about John Henry. His gelding would be the first to know if there was a wolf nearby, so Decker would be the second.

"I guess I'll take my chances."

"Well, you'll be okay as long as it doesn't rain."

The ground outside had looked fairly dry to Decker as he rode in.

"Expecting rain?"

"That's what my bad leg tells me."

"How reliable is your bad leg?"

The man shrugged. "Half and half, I guess," he admitted.

"I'll buck those odds," Decker said. He finished the beer and said, "Thanks."

"Sure."

"Anyplace I can get some supplies?"

"First tent as you came into town. There's no sign on it, but it's the closest to a general store as we got."

"Thanks again."

Decker turned to leave, then decided to go ahead and ask the question. He'd gotten everything he could out of the man, so if he clammed up now it wouldn't matter.

"By the way, I'm looking for a man you may have seen hereabouts."

"Oh? Who's that?"

"He's called the Baron."

It might have been Decker's imagination, but it seemed to get quiet in the room.

He was watching the bartender's eyes closely when he said the name. Although a man can control the expression on his face most of the time, the eyes usually get away from him. He was sure that he saw a glint of recognition in the man's eyes.

"The Baron? Is that his name?"

"That's what he's called."

"What's he look like?"

Decker gave the man the information that was on the poster in his pocket.

"Can't say I've seen a man who matches that description," the bartender said. "Sorry I can't help you."

"You've helped enough," Decker said. "Thanks anyway."

Decker had decided not to push the man. It was enough that he knew the Baron. It meant Decker wasn't wasting his time up here.

As Decker started for the door he noticed a disturbance at the table of five men where the big lumberjack was sitting. The two men on either side of him suddenly grabbed his arms, and one of the other men leaned over and punched him in the face. It was so sudden that Decker stopped to watch.

The man who had thrown the blow was off balance, so there wasn't much force behind it. The big lumberman simply shook it off and then rose to a standing position, roaring, taking the men who were holding his arms with him. Both men, looking frightened, held on for dear life as the big man swung both of them around, dragging them over the table and slamming them into each other.

The table collapsed beneath the weight, and the other two men jumped back.

The big man waited for the two fallen men to regain their feet, and then he faced all four, two of whom had picked up pieces of the collapsed table.

"You fellas are making a big mistake," the man said. "Put the lumber down and go on back to your camp."

"We're gonna splatter your brains," one of them said, and the others nodded in agreement.

The four moved toward the bigger man, and he swung a backhanded blow that almost took one of their heads off. The other three swarmed over him, two of them swinging the wood. The big man blocked the blows with his huge arms, then grabbed both of the wood-wielding men by the jacket fronts and began to shake them. Decker knew their brains had to be bouncing back and forth inside their heads.

Decker then saw the fourth man take out a knife. He began to circle the big man so he could come up from behind. Everybody in the room saw what was happening, but no one made a move to do anything. That was when Decker moved.

Decker came up on the man from behind, grabbed his wrist, and twisted. As the man staggered off balance, Decker broke the man's forearm with a satisfying, audible snap.

The big man slammed the two men he was holding together, this time banging their heads. As one of the men slumped forward, the bigger man released him and let him fall to the floor. He held the other man up, pounded his big fist into his face once, and then released him.

As he faced Decker, Decker put his hands up in front of him and said, "Take it easy. I'm on your side."

The big man looked down at the man who was cradling his broken arm and saw the knife on the floor in front of him.

"So I see. I'm in your debt."

"Don't mention it. You want to hold these fellas for the law?"

"Ain't none," the man said. "Why don't we just get out of here and leave them to themselves."

"Good idea."

They went outside and Decker moved to take hold of John Henry's reins.

"This your horse?"

"He is."

"He's a mighty good-looking animal."

"Thank you."

Decker took a moment to examine his

new acquaintance. He was big, wearing a plaid coat with a fur collar and a fur hat. He had a full beard and was obviously a lumberjack.

"Looks a little long in the tooth, though."

"John Henry's nine, but there's plenty of fire left in him. He's better than any horse half his age."

"I'll bet. Name's Frenchie," the man said, extending a huge hand.

"Frenchie?" Decker said, shaking the man's hand. "You don't sound French."

"I ain't, but every lumber camp's gotta have a Frenchie, right?"

"I guess so," Decker agreed, amused by the man. "Who were those fellas?"

"Just some fellas from another lumber camp. They took exception to something I said."

"What was that?"

"I told them any man from my camp could whip any three men from theirs."

"Well, you proved that point."

"With your help."

"Ah," Decker said, "but I took care of the fourth man."

"That's right," the man said. "You did. Are you just passing through?"

"Yes. I was just going to get some supplies."

"First tent as you come into town," Frenchie said. "Going that way myself. Mind if I walk along?"

"Not at all," Decker said. The man appeared to be genuinely friendly, but Decker stayed on the alert nevertheless.

They walked together, John Henry trailing behind them. Decker held the reins loosely in his left hand, keeping his right hand free.

When they entered the tent the bounty hunter saw that supplies were stacked on the dirt floor and that a counter had been set up similar to the one used as a bar in the saloon tent. Behind the counter was a man who couldn't have been more than five and a half feet tall but who had the upper body of a man a full foot taller.

"Hello, Frenchie."

"Ballantine," Frenchie said. "Meet my friend . . ."

"Decker."

"Pleased to meet you, Decker. What can I do for you today?"

"I'm passing through and I need a few things."

"Well, just name 'em."

Decker reeled off the supplies he needed: some coffee, beef jerky, and some canned peaches.

"I got 'em all," Ballantine said. "Just hang

on a second while I find 'em. This is sure gonna be easier when I get me a regular store."

"See what you can do for me, too, Ballantine," Frenchie said, handing the small man a list.

Ballantine nodded and went off to take care of both of them.

"Sounds like a nice setup," Decker said because he didn't know what else to say.

"Where you gonna be spending the night, Decker?"

"On the trail somewhere, I guess. The 'hotel tent' didn't sound very comfortable."

Frenchie made a face and said, "It ain't. We got a lot more room up at camp, and all the tents have potbellied stoves in 'em. You're welcome to spend the night there if you like — and you'll get a hot meal. We got a great cook in camp."

Decker studied Frenchie, wondering if the man was genuinely friendly enough to extend the hospitality of his camp to a stranger. His natural cynicism made it hard for Decker to believe that, but looking into the guileless face of his new acquaintance, he was almost persuaded to change his mind. The man seemed for all the world like a big, friendly teddy bear.

"That's real hospitable of you. Do you

have that authority? I mean, to invite strang-
ers to camp —"

"I'm not *the* foreman, but I'm a crew
leader. That gives me some rights, I guess.
I'm sure the foreman and the owner won't
mind — especially Miz Boone. She's a real
hospitable lady."

"Is she the foreman or the owner?"

Frenchie found that real funny, and when
he finished laughing he said, "She's the
owner, by God. The foreman's Big Jeff
Reno."

"Big?"

Frenchie nodded and smiled, "Bigger'n
me. If he don't want you there, he'll just
toss you off the mountain."

"I got your coffee, Frenchie," Ballantine
said, returning with Decker's supplies in
hand. "You want to bring your wagon
around back?"

"Well," Decker said, "I look forward to
meeting him."

In the final analysis, it was the mention of
the potbellied stove that did it, the bounty
hunter had to admit to himself as they left
the store.

CHAPTER TEN

As Decker helped Frenchie load the wagon, he found the man's strength to be incredible. The burly man easily lifted objects that most men would find impossible to move. When the wagon was loaded, Decker tied John Henry to the back of the buckboard and climbed into the seat next to Frenchie.

"What is it you do for a living, Decker?"

Decker hesitated for a moment but finally decided to answer honestly.

"I'm a bounty hunter."

"For real?" Frenchie asked, looking at him wide-eyed.

"Yep, for real."

"That's better than being a real lawman, ain't it?"

"I guess —"

"I mean, real lawmen capture outlaws and don't get to collect the bounty, right?"

"That's right."

"Who gets it?"

"Nobody."

"So, if you catch the outlaw, you get the bounty, right?"

"That's right."

"That's a lot of money sometimes, isn't it?"

"Sometimes."

"Is it hard work?"

"Real hard."

"But I'll bet you're good at it, ain't you?"

"Yes," Decker said.

"You up here hunting somebody?"

"Yes."

"Who?"

Decker didn't answer that one.

"I guess that was a stupid question, huh?"

"Not stupid . . . exactly."

"Yeah, it was dumb. I'm sorry. I'm just a real curious fella."

"And friendly."

"Oh yeah. Some people say I'm too friendly. You think that's possible?"

"For some people, I guess not."

"You seem like a real friendly guy. You mean you ain't, really?"

"Not so you'd notice," Decker said.

"You got friends, right?"

"Some."

"Then that makes you a friendly fella. Hell, everybody's got friends."

"I guess so."

"Hey, I got an idea!" Frenchie said, suddenly excited.

"What?"

"Maybe I could help you find whoever you're trying to catch."

"I don't think —"

"Is he up here somewhere?"

"All I know is that he's somewhere in the Powder River area."

"Lot of area to cover," Frenchie said. "I bet you could use some help."

"I usually work alone, Frenchie."

"Alone, huh?"

Decker nodded, and Frenchie shrugged.

"Ah, I guess I belong up here cutting down trees."

"I'll bet you're good at it."

"Damn good."

"Then I guess you should do what you do best, and I should do what I do best."

Frenchie thought about that for a moment, then started laughing.

"Hell," he said, banging Decker on the back hard enough to bruise him, "that's damn near the nicest I ever been turned down."

"What was the nicest?"

"Well, there was this little gal once . . ."

■ ■ ■ ■

When they pulled into camp Decker immediately noticed a man he assumed was Big Jeff Reno.

"That Reno?"

"That's him."

As big as Frenchie was — and he surely topped six-three — he was dwarfed by Reno, who had to be six foot eight and probably outweighed the big logger by fifty pounds.

"Jesus," Decker said.

"I told you, he's a big man."

The woman standing next to Reno was young and pretty, and it was no insult to her that Decker didn't notice her right away. Reno was the kind of man who dominated any scene, no matter who was there.

"That's Miz Boone," Frenchie said. "She took over the camp when her father was killed."

"Accident?"

"Nope," Frenchie said, giving Decker a sideways look. "He was murdered."

"Murdered?"

"Shot in the head."

"When?"

"A couple of weeks ago."

"Anybody arrested?"

"No," Frenchie said. "There's no law here, Decker. We sent word for a federal marshal."

"Who's working Wyoming-Montana?" Decker asked.

"Fella named Murdock. Heard of him?"

Decker thought he had and nodded.

"Anyway, we don't know when he'll get here."

"By the time he does the trail will be even colder than it is now."

"It's sad," Frenchie said. "Jack Boone was a good man."

As the wagon entered the center of the camp both Reno and the Boone woman looked their way. Frenchie stopped the wagon just in front of them and hopped down.

"Who's that?" Reno asked immediately.

"A new friend of mine," Frenchie told them. "Name's Decker. He's passing through and needs a place to stay. I offered him a bunk in my tent. Okay?"

Reno studied Decker, who had stepped down, and then looked at Miss Boone. She, too, was studying the bounty hunter intently.

"Do you vouch for him, Frenchie?" she asked.

"Sure, I vouch for him, Miz Boone."

"All right, then," she said. "Why not?"

"Thank you, ma'am," Decker said.

She looked at him as if she was surprised that he had spoken, then turned and walked away. There was one wooden cabin in the camp, and she walked to it and entered. Decker recalled what Frenchie had said about everybody being friendly and having friends, and he decided to give her the benefit of the doubt. After all, her father had been killed just two weeks earlier.

Later, Decker would berate himself for being too dumb to see what was coming.

The bounty hunter had to agree with what Frenchie had said about the camp's cook. Either he was one of the best cooks whose wares Decker had ever tasted or food simply tasted better when the air was cold.

Decker had been left to his own devices in the mess tent and was drawing curious looks from the loggers around him. Frenchie was nowhere to be found until he suddenly stepped into the tent with Jeff Reno. They were deep in conversation, and once or twice Reno looked Decker's way, nodding.

It might have dawned on Decker then, but he was too interested in the hot food in front of him.

When Frenchie and Reno finally finished

their conversation, Frenchie got himself a bowl of stew, then sat next to Decker. He attacked his food with vigor and spoke to Decker between bites.

"Well, my friend, how do you like the food?"

"Just like you said," Decker told him.

"Ah, I knew you'd enjoy it."

"I hope I didn't get you in trouble with your boss."

"Big Jeff?" Frenchie said. "No, we're good friends. Whatever I do is all right with him."

"I'm glad to hear it."

"How have the lads here been treating you?"

"Like I had the plague."

"Ah," Frenchie said, slapping his forehead with the palm of his hand. "I should have known!"

"Known what?"

"That they would be suspicious of a stranger in their midst only a couple of weeks after Jack Boone was shot."

"Speaking of Boone," Decker said, "what is Miss Boone's first name?"

"Dani."

"Danny?"

Frenchie spelled the name for Decker and then said, "I think it's short for Danielle."

"Pretty name."

"She was all bundled up when you saw her, but take my word for it, she's a pretty little thing."

"How old is she?"

"I'm not sure, I guess about twenty, twenty-one."

"That's young to be running an operation like this, isn't it?"

"That's why she's leaning heavily on Big Jeff and . . ." Frenchie let the sentence trail off without finishing it.

"And you?"

"A lot of us," Frenchie said, obviously avoiding the question.

Decker looked Frenchie in the eye and said, "Why is it I get the feeling you're a little more in charge here than you let on?"

Frenchie put down his fork and looked at Decker.

"I ain't in charge, Decker," Frenchie said. "Reno's in charge, and he reports to Miz Boone. I was just good friends with her father, that's all. She respects that."

"Frenchie," Decker said, "why did you ask me up here? Really?"

"Finish eating," Frenchie said. "Dani would like to see you in her cabin — if you've a mind to talk to her."

"I'll talk to her," Decker said. "And then I'll talk to you — or you'll talk to me."

"You've got a deal," Frenchie said, and once again he attacked his meal.

Chapter Eleven

After they finished eating, Frenchie led Decker to Dani Boone's cabin.

"Are you coming in?" Decker said.

"Nope. This is between you and her."

Decker knocked, and when the young woman opened the door he noticed two things. Number one, she was indeed extremely pretty, as Frenchie had said. Her hair was chestnut colored and hung down past her shoulders. She was wearing a heavy plaid work shirt that did nothing to hide the proud thrust of her full breasts. And her jeans molded themselves to the curve of her hips.

The second thing he noticed was the scent of coffee in the cabin.

"Would you like some coffee?" she asked.

"Please."

"Come in, then," she said, stepping back.

He entered and found himself in a cluttered room dominated by a huge table that was covered with papers. Off in one corner was a cot, and on a potbellied stove sat a pot of coffee.

"Take off your jacket," she said, "and have a seat. We have something to talk about."

There was no note of hospitality in her voice, and her expression was stern. She had sent for him, and she had expected him to come.

Then she walked to him and handed Decker a cup of coffee.

Accepting the hot cup gratefully, he asked, "Who says we have something to talk about, Miss Boone?"

"Frenchie does."

"Do you listen to everything Frenchie says?"

"My father trusted Frenchie completely," she said. "If Frenchie had taken the job, he'd be foreman instead of Reno."

"How does Reno feel about that?"

"He knows it and accepts it."

"I don't know how a man can accept knowing that if another man wanted his job, he'd have it."

"Reno does," she said with certainty. "But I didn't send for you to discuss my business."

"You didn't send for me at all, Miss Boone," he said. "As I understood it, you *asked* me to come here and talk."

She closed her eyes for a moment, then opened them and said, "Yes, of course. I'm sorry."

"All right, then. What does Frenchie say we have to talk about?"

"You know that my father was killed two weeks ago?" she asked sadly.

"Frenchie told me."

"We believe that a hired killed did it."

"I see," Decker said, and he was starting to. Frenchie was in the saloon tent when Decker asked the bartender about the Baron. After that, Frenchie took a sudden interest in John Henry, which allowed him to meet Decker.

"Who do you think did the hiring?"

"I have no idea. That's what I want to find out."

"What's that got to do with me?"

"Frenchie says you're a bounty hunter."

"So."

"He says you're the best at what you do."

"That's a lot to say about someone you've just met."

"He says he's heard of you."

"That's news to me."

"Decker, I would like to hire you to find the man who killed my father, then find out who hired him. I'll pay you well."

"Sounds like a job for a Pinkerton detective, not a bounty hunter."

"You have more at stake here than a Pinkerton detective would have."

"Like what?"

"You're already looking for the man."

"Am I?"

"We believe that the man who was hired to kill my father was the Baron."

"I see," Decker said thoughtfully. "So that's why Frenchie told me I could stay here."

"I apologize for his bringing you up here on false pretenses."

"He didn't, really. He promised me a meal and a place to sleep. I'll have those, won't I?"

"Of course."

"Even if I don't accept your job?"

She bit her lip before answering. "Of course."

Decker sipped his coffee, considering what had happened. No matter how you looked at it, Frenchie had lured him up here on false pretenses, but Decker was not the kind of man whose feelings bruised easily. In fact, he felt vindicated that he had questioned Frenchie's apparent friendliness and had now been proven right.

"Your father's been dead two weeks, Miss

Boone," Decker pointed out. "Seems to me the trail is pretty cold."

"You and I both know that the Baron is up here somewhere around the Powder River."

"Why would he take a job so close to where he hangs his hat?"

"I have no idea."

"What makes you think that he's the one who killed your father?"

"It would take the best to kill my father," she said.

"That's fine, Miss Boone. It makes a nice epitaph, but what proof do you have?"

"I don't . . . have any real proof."

Decker stood up and put his empty cup down.

"Miss Boone, I can't accept your offer. It would constitute a conflict of interest."

"But you're already hunting for him."

"If that's true, then when I find him and bring him in, I'll be paid."

"Look," Dani Boone said, "maybe I'm not doing this right. Maybe I'm not asking nicely enough, but I'm not used to asking for anything."

"Maybe you should learn how, then."

She compressed her lips and then said, "Maybe I should."

Decker walked to the door and then turned.

"In return for your hospitality," he said, "if I find the Baron, I'll question him about your father's death. Anything I find out, I'll relay to you. Is that to your satisfaction?"

She thought a moment and then, not looking happy, said, "I guess it will have to be, won't it?"

Decker nodded and left. Outside, he wondered why he had given her such a hard time and why he had gotten a certain amount of satisfaction from it.

CHAPTER TWELVE

Outside, Frenchie was waiting for Decker.

"Well?" he asked.

"If you weren't so much bigger than me I'd take a poke at you."

"And I'd deserve it," Frenchie said. "But my guess is, if you were that mad, my size wouldn't stop you."

"You're right."

"Did you agree?"

"No."

"What?"

"I won't work for her."

"Why not?"

"Because I work for myself, Frenchie. That's one of the reasons I do what I do."

Frenchie hesitated a moment, then said, "I can understand that."

"Good."

"You want some coffee?"

"You wouldn't have something a little stronger, would you?"

"As a matter of fact," Frenchie said, "I would."

Frenchie took Decker to a tent where there was a five-handed poker game going, and another man watching it. The tent was filled with smoke.

"What's this?"

"This is where we come to relax if we don't want to go into town."

He led Decker past the game to a make-shift three-foot bar in the back.

"Can't offer you much of a variety," Frenchie said, reaching behind the bar. "We've got rotgut, and more rotgut."

"I'll take it," Decker said. He took a swig from the bottle and felt it warm his insides instantly, like liquid fire. He handed it to Frenchie, and the big logger took a huge swallow.

"So, what's the story?" Frenchie asked.

"If I hear anything I think she should know, I'll tell her," Decker said.

"That's all?"

"That's all."

"And she went for it?"

"She wasn't about to get any more."

"She's one stubborn woman, you know."

"She's hardly a woman."

"Well, she ain't no kid, you could tell that by looking at her."

"And just what is she to you?"

"Mmm, I'm sort of like an uncle."

"An uncle who calls her 'Miz Boone'?"

"She's also my boss."

"Did she work here with her father?"

"No," Frenchie said. "She lived in the East, but she was on her way here when he was killed."

"He was dead when she got here?"

"Yes," Frenchie said. "She arrived the day after he was killed. They hadn't seen each other for five years, and they hadn't parted on the best of terms. This was supposed to be a reconciliation."

"I see."

"Do you? She feels real guilty about her father's death. She wants to catch the man who did it, and the man who ordered it." Frenchie leaned on the bar and said, "I guess you figured out by now that I heard you asking about the Baron in the bar. I thought you might be able to help her. When I met you, and heard who you were, I knew you were the man we needed."

"You knew —"

"Look, I don't care if you help her on her terms, or on your terms. All I care about is that you help her."

"Just so you know," Decker said, "that my main concern is not to help anyone but

103

myself."

Frenchie put his huge paw on Decker's shoulder and said, "I'll bet even you don't believe that."

"I still think you should let me ride along with you," Frenchie said.

It was morning, and Decker was getting ready to ride out. He had the supplies he'd bought at the "general store" plus a few things that Frenchie had thrown in.

Decker was astride John Henry, while Frenchie was standing at his side. Off to one side Big Jeff Reno was watching, and from the look on the man's face Decker knew the foreman didn't wish him luck. In front of the lone cabin in camp stood Dani Boone, her face expressionless.

"I think you'd do better to stay around here and keep an eye on things, Frenchie."

"What do you mean?" Frenchie asked.

Decker looked at Reno and Dani again, and then back at his new friend.

"I don't know. Just a feeling I have. While I'm gone, be more of an uncle than an employee, eh?"

"While you're gone?" Frenchie asked. "Does that mean you plan on coming back?"

"Plans are made to be broken," Decker

said. "I'll be seeing you."

Decker rode out of the lumber camp, wondering how whoever had hired the Baron to kill Jack Boone felt about Dani Boone coming in to run things.

CHAPTER THIRTEEN

Farther up the river, in a town named Broadus, the man who called himself Brand — but whom others called the Baron — rolled over in bed and came into contact with a warm female body.

Brand looked at the woman who was lying next to him. She was a big woman, with long black hair and a broad, very sexy behind. He slapped it loudly.

"Hey!" he said as her head snapped up.

"What?"

"Breakfast!"

"Oh, Lord," she said, rolling over. Her front was just as impressive as her back. Her name was Josephine Hale. "My head is killing me."

"That will teach you to try and drink like a man," Brand said.

"Can all Russians hold their liquor as well as you can?" she asked.

"Yes," he said. "Russians are famous for

their ability to drink — and eat. Breakfast, woman!"

"I'm getting it, I'm getting it," she said, jumping out of bed. He watched her as she walked naked across the floor, acres of bare flesh sprouting goose bumps until she slipped into a robe.

"Eggs and bacon?" she asked.

"For a start."

"Oh, Jesus," she said. "It's going to be one of those mornings. Flapjacks and sausages, too?"

"Yes."

"How can you eat so much the night after you've drunk so much?" she asked, shaking her head as she left the room.

Brand reclined on the bed, hands behind his head, and thought about his little hideaway on the Powder River.

He had found Broadus quite by accident. What he had been looking for was a part of the United States that had a climate similar to Russia's. Montana filled the bill, especially in the winter. Finding Montana, he had then found Broadus, and there he found Josephine.

Josephine owned a store in town that sold women's clothing, and she owned a small house that she lived in alone. That is, she lived there alone when Brand was away.

She didn't know what Brand did when he wasn't in Broadus, and she didn't care. All she cared about was that when he was finished he came back to her.

Montana, Broadus, and Josephine had come to mean a lot to Brand, which was the reason he'd decided never to ply his trade in Montana.

He smelled the bacon grease as it hit the pan, and he got up. When he dressed he did not bother to strap on his gun.

He often wondered what the townspeople would say — and what Josephine would say — if they ever found out that he was the hired killer known as the Baron.

Sometimes he wished he could take Josephine up on her offer to simply live off what she made at the store, but he knew he'd never be able to do that. He was in too deep ever to do that — and besides, in a year the store could never bring in what he could make from one job.

Of course, all he ever did with his money was put it in the Bank of Broadus, but it pleased him to know that it was there. If anything ever happened to him, if he didn't return one day from a job, the money would go to Josephine.

She didn't know about that, and she'd never find out until after he was dead.

As he left the bedroom the smell of coffee mingled with that of the bacon, and his mouth watered as he entered the kitchen.

"Is it ready?" he asked, seating himself at the table.

Josephine turned away from the stove, a cup of coffee in her hand. She set it down in front of him, kissed him, and said, "Anybody ever tell you that you were too demanding?"

"I have never had any complaints from my other women," he said as she returned to the stove.

"Ha!" Josephine said over her shoulder. "I happen to know that no other woman would have you. No other woman would put up with your kind of behavior."

She often wondered, however, whether or not he had other women in other parts of the country. He was never gone for much more than a month or two at a time, but he was sometimes away several times a year. At least that meant that even if he had other women, he spent most of his time with her.

For Josephine, that was enough.

She knew that she was a big woman, and that most men had trouble measuring up to her. She also knew that although she might have been described as "handsome," she was certainly no beauty.

Brand had been one of the few men who hadn't been intimidated by her or put off by her. Many other men had wanted her, she knew, for one night, just to see what it would be like, but Brand had never been like that. In fact, he had known her for months before he had even tried to kiss her.

No, although she had had affairs with a few men Brand was the only man for her, and even if he *had* found it necessary to have other women, she would be satisfied with the time he gave her.

She did still wonder, though, what sort of business took him away for those long periods at a time.

She wondered, but she had never asked.

And she never would.

CHAPTER FOURTEEN

The first night Decker camped on the trail after leaving the Boone lumber camp made him appreciate Frenchie's offer of hospitality — whatever the man's motives — even more. Sitting in front of his fire, he pulled his jacket closer around him and put his fur collar up to ward off the chill. As it turned out, being cold saved his life, because it was when he leaned over to grab his blanket and wrap himself in it that the shot was fired — missing him by inches.

After the first shot he rolled away from the fire as quickly as he could and drew his gun. It was in situations like this that Decker wished he were a better shot with a handgun. His cut-down shotgun had a limited effective range, and was of almost no use in instances like this. True, he could have fired into the brush, and his double-O shot would cover a wide area, its pattern spreading more the farther it went, but at some point

— when it spread too much — it became in effective.

Decker looked over at his rifle on the other side of the fire. He had rolled away from the fire instinctively, trying to get out of its light, but in doing so had also rolled farther away from the rifle.

Anxiously, he looked at John Henry, who seemed unconcerned about the goings-on. Had he been ambushing someone he would have gone for the horse first, either to free it or kill it. He was relieved that his ambusher — or ambushers — had not thought of that yet.

They might, though, which gave him three possible choices. He could stay where he was, but that wasn't such a great choice. He might be away from most of the fire's light, but he was still out in the open.

The second choice was to move over by John Henry, to protect the horse, but then he'd still be waiting for them to make a move.

His third choice was to move into the brush himself, out of sight, which would put him on more equal footing with his at-tackers.

Lying on his belly, trying to make himself as inconspicuous as possible, Decker wondered why there had only been that one shot. As if to answer his question there were suddenly two more, sounding as if they had been fired from two different guns. Each kicked up some dirt on either side of him, and he knew he had to move or he'd be dead in seconds.

He took a deep breath, then rose and ran for the brush. Three or four more shots rang out, narrowly missing him, and then he wasn't out in the open anymore.

He stopped when he had cover and crouched down, staying perfectly still. He listened intently, trying desperately to hear something that would give away the position of his assailants.

"Jesus, we missed —" he heard, and then someone said, "Shhh!" forcefully.

That was enough for him to pinpoint their position. He started to move through the brush, hoping to come up behind them before it occurred to them to go after his horse.

As he moved along, Decker started to wonder if he wasn't getting a little old for this business. The two men had managed to get close enough to take a shot at him without his hearing them. This was just another in a series of lapses he had noticed since he had started out after the Baron. Even the usually reliable John Henry had not detected the presence of the men before they could fire. Decker wondered if the cold had affected the horse's sense of smell and hearing. Maybe it had even affected his.

Why couldn't the Baron have hid out in Mexico, like a lot of other outlaws? he wondered.

After he moved about a hundred yards in a semicircle Decker stopped and listened again. This time when he heard them they were much closer.

"Where did he go?" one man asked.

"I told you to keep your mouth shut!" a second voice said.

They were about ten yards to his left and in front of him.

He moved cautiously, not wanting to alert them, and when he thought he was directly behind them he decided on his course of action. If he called out to them they could split up and would immediately gain the advantage. He was better off taking a more direct course.

He raised his sawed-off and fired both barrels ahead of him. While the men screamed in anguish he quickly ejected the two empty shells and replaced them.

He moved forward then, gun held out ahead of him, and approached what had become a stream of steady moans.

"God, Jesus!" one man yelled. "I been cut in half!"

The other was simply groaning, holding himself with both arms.

Decker moved to the shouting man, but as he leaned over him the man stopped yelling. An instant later he emitted a sound that could only be a death rattle. This man would never give him any trouble again, Decker knew.

He turned to approach the other man, whose wounds appeared less serious. Still, he was surprised when the man rolled over with a gun in his hand. Without even thinking, Decker squeezed off one barrel, striking the man in the face, obliterating it totally.

There was an eerie silence after the shots, and Decker checked both men again. From his vantage point he had a clear look at his campfire. If they had been better marksmen — or if he had not been so cold — he would be dead now instead of them.

Decker was about to step out into the open when there was a shot from the opposite side of the campfire.

"Shit!" Decker said, hitting the ground. Apparently these men had not been alone but were simply the first wave.

Decker rolled over, removed the spent

shells from his gun, and loaded two more. It was at times like this — and a lot of others — that he wished he was a competent shot with a six-shooter, simply because they had six shots.

"Dave!" a voice called out. "Steve!"

Well, now Decker knew the names of the two dead men. Of course, that still didn't tell him who they were.

Keeping low, Decker crept over one of the bodies, intending to move back into the brush, but he stopped short. He holstered his gun, picked up one of the dead men's rifles, and then began to circle to his right, facing the campfire. Maybe whoever was on the other side — one man? two? — would think that Decker was as dead as his two friends, and step out into the open.

Moving slowly but steadily, Decker heard someone say, "Shit!" under his breath, and he followed the sound of the voice.

He was opposite the place where he'd left the two bodies when someone suddenly shouted, "Hey, Steve! You hit?"

Decker started, because the voice came from right in front of him, about ten feet away. Decker could see that the man was wearing a plaid jacket and heavy pants. From the look of him, he was a lumberjack — an interesting point.

Peering through the brush, he saw a lone man lying on his stomach, a rifle in his hand. He came up behind the man, who heard him too late.

"Freeze," Decker said, putting the barrel of his rifle right against the man's ass. "Let's have a talk."

"I got nothing to say."

"We can talk now, or I give you another asshole and *then* we can talk."

"Jesus! Wait —"

"All right, then," Decker said. "Toss your rifle out into the clearing."

The man obeyed, flinging the rifle away from him.

"Who sent you?"

"I don't know."

"What the hell —" Decker said, pressing the rifle butt harder against the man's ass.

"I mean it," he said. "I just came along for the ride."

"And the money?"

"Sure. And the money."

Decker backed away from the man and said, "Okay, roll over. I want to take a look at you."

The man rolled over and Decker saw his hand inside his jacket. Before the man had time to bring the gun out, Decker fired. The bullet struck the man in the throat, bringing a gusher of blood from his mouth, and then he slumped back with his eyes still open.

"Damn!" Decker said.

He moved through the brush until he found a branch approximately the size and thickness of his arm, then walked to his campfire and lit one end of it. Using it as a torch he went back to check the first two bodies. He did not recognize either of the men, but he did recognize the way they were dressed.

There was no doubt in his mind that all three men were loggers.

As he drank some strong black coffee, Decker pondered on the significance of the attack. Someone from a logging camp had sent those two men after him, and the only logging camp he'd been anywhere near was the Boone camp.

Who was really in command there? he wondered. How much real authority did Dani Boone have? She had just taken over from her father. How much loyalty would she command from her men? And why, if she was so anxious for Decker to find her father's killer, would she send two men to kill him.

No, it wasn't Dani Boone.

The logic that eliminated Dani Boone, however, did not apply to the other person who was in authority: Big Jeff Reno. Decker had had no contact whatsoever with Reno during the short time he'd been in the camp, yet whenever the man looked at him, it had been with distinct displeasure.

Why? What could Reno have against him? Perhaps Reno recognized Decker. It wasn't impossible that Decker had once brought in or killed a relative of his. Decker couldn't count the times that someone's brother or father or wife or even daughter had tried to kill him out of revenge.

Still, if he'd had some contact with a relative of Reno's in the past, and if there had been any resemblance at all, surely he'd remember.

Was he leaving someone out? What about Frenchie? If he'd been so close to Dani's father, wouldn't he have some authority with the men? He could have given the order, but it had been Frenchie who'd brought Decker into camp in the first place.

Reno was Decker's choice, but he decided not to go back to camp now and find out. He could do that later. It would be some time before Reno knew that his men had failed, and by that time it would be too late to send anyone else after him.

Decker fed some more mesquite into the fire, then lay back with his head on his pillow. He'd sleep lightly tonight. He filed Jeff Reno away in the back of his mind as unfinished business.

Back in Douglas, Wyoming, Sheriff Calder was sitting in his office, wondering how long he would remain sheriff there.

He hadn't heard from the Baron in some time, and he was beginning to wonder if Decker hadn't actually found him and brought him in — or killed him. Without the Baron to back him up, Calder wouldn't be able to hold on to Douglas. As soon as the news broke that the notorious hired killer had been brought in, the town would turn on him.

Nervous, the sheriff tried to calm himself. He knew what the Baron was capable of. Before he panicked, he'd wait until he either heard from him or heard that he'd been caught.

In Broadus, Brand realized that it had been a while since he had contacted Calder to find out if anyone was asking about his services.

He was sitting on the porch of Josephine's house, waiting for her to close the store and come home to cook him dinner. It wouldn't take long for him to walk over to the telegraph office and send word, but that would tell Calder where he was. What he usually did was travel to a different town to contact the sheriff. That way no two messages ever came from the same place.

Right now he was too comfortable to saddle a horse and ride to the next town, so he just settled back and continued to wait for Jo.

CHAPTER FIFTEEN

Broadus was by far the largest town Decker had come across along the Powder River. It had not one, but two hotels, two saloons, a telegraph office, and many other shops that only show up in a growing town. To his surprise, it even had an ice cream parlor.

Decker found the livery and gave John Henry over to the liveryman's care. He was happy to be in a real town again, where he'd be able to get a real meal and sleep in a real bed. Although his stay at the logging camp had been comfortable enough, it would not be able to rival a stay in a true town.

He entered the hotel lobby, put his saddlebags on the floor, and leaned his rifle against the front of the desk.

There was no clerk, but just moments later a man stepped out from behind a curtained doorway. He was a small, rather portly man with thinning black hair and a small moustache.

"May I help you, sir?" he inquired politely.

"Yes, I'd like a room."

"Certainly. Please sign the register."

While he was signing, Decker asked, "Who's the sheriff here?"

"Our sheriff's name is Kyle Roman, sir."

"How long has he been sheriff?"

"I'd say . . . almost two years."

"Is he a good one?"

"I'd say he was quite adequate."

"Adequate" was not a word Decker would use to describe a lawman. He was either good or bad — and if he was adequate, that was the same as being bad. Still, two years seemed long enough for the man to know the area.

Decker finished signing in and asked for a room that did not overlook the street.

"Of course, sir," the clerk said. "Here you are."

He gave Decker the key and told him the room number.

"Do you have bath facilities?" the bounty hunter asked.

"Oh, yes, sir. If you go out the front door, make a left, and then another left, we have a bathhouse at the rear of the hotel."

"Thanks," Decker said.

He went to his room, dropped off his gear, and then followed the clerk's directions to

123

the bathhouse. Inside, he found bathing facilities for almost a dozen people. Three of the stalls were in use.

"A bath, sir?" an elderly man asked. He was sweating, because it was oppressively hot inside the building.

"That's why I'm here," Decker announced, feeling himself begin to sweat.

"Please undress out here and hang your clothing on a hook."

"Out here?"

"Don't worry, sir. Everything will still be here when you come out."

Decker, looking dubious, undressed and accepted a towel from the man, which he wrapped around his middle.

"You can have stall number 7, sir. The water is plenty hot."

Decker picked up his gunbelt and headed for the back.

"Oh, sir, you can leave your gun out here."

"Maybe I can," Decker said, "but I sure as hell won't."

The man didn't know how to react to that.

"P-Please," he stammered. "It's the rules —" Decker ignored him and kept going, closing the door behind him.

The stall was a little larger than a jail cell. The tub was made of white porcelain, and the water was as hot as promised. There was no chair in the stall, so Decker was forced to leave his holster on the floor, but in a place where he'd still be able to get at it.

Decker soaped himself down, and after he rinsed off he simply lay back and allowed the heat to soak into his tired body. He realized that he had almost fallen asleep in that position when he heard the door to his stall open.

In an instant he had his gun in his hand, but a voice said to him, "There's no need for that."

The voice was mild and unhurried, and Decker turned his head to see who it belonged to. The man was standing just inside the door, his thumbs hooked into the front of his belt. He was tall and stocky and wore a star on his chest. Seeing that there was no threat to him, Decker put his gun back on the floor. The man's beard and mustache made it tough to figure out his age.

"Sheriff Roman, I presume."

"That's right," the sheriff said, moving farther into the stall. "How'd you know my name?"

"I asked about you at the hotel."

"And I asked about you at the hotel," Roman said. "You scared old Billy when you broke the rules and brought your gun in here."

"Sorry about that, Sheriff, but I don't go very many places without my gun."

Roman cocked an eyebrow and asked, "On the run, are you?"

"No. My name is Decker. I'm a bounty hunter."

"Ah, I see," Roman said. "You must have a lot of trouble with people looking for revenge."

"Some."

"Some," Roman repeated derisively. "A man like you —"

"What do you know about a man like me?"

"I've heard of you, Decker," Roman said. "You're good, or so they say."

When Decker didn't support or deny the statement, Roman continued. "What are you doing in Broadus?"

"Maybe we could talk someplace else." Decker said. "After my bath."

"Yeah, I guess this is sort of awkward."

"The reason I was asking for you was that I was going to come and see you after my bath and discuss what I'm doing here. Does that suit you?"

"That suits me."

"Fine. Can I get on with my bath now?"

"Sure . . . but give me your gun."

"No."

"I could take it from you," Roman said, indicating his badge.

"I wouldn't want you to try."

They stared at each other for a moment, and then Roman said, "In my office, after your bath."

"See you there," Decker told him and fished around at the bottom of the tub for the soap.

CHAPTER SIXTEEN

Roman was seated behind his desk, drinking a cup of coffee, when Decker entered the office.

"Grab yourself a cup," he said. "The pot's a fresh one."

Decker did so, then took the chair in front of the sheriff's desk. The office was small, but it was clean and well cared for.

Sitting so close to Roman, Decker realized the lawman was younger than he was. The beard made him look older, but Decker didn't think the man was yet thirty.

"So?" Roman said.

"I'm looking for a man," Decker told him.

"That's what you do," Roman said. "What's this particular man's name?"

"He's called the Baron."

"The hired gun?"

"That's him."

"What makes you think he's here?"

"I don't know if he's in Broadus," Decker

said. "The word I got was that he was up here around the Powder River somewhere."

"Know what he looks like?"

"Just what it says on his paper," Decker said. He handed the poster to Roman.

"I must have a copy of this somewhere," the sheriff muttered, accepting the poster.

He read it, then passed it back.

"From that description he could be anyone."

"The talk about him says he's foreign. Comes from Russia or someplace," Decker said. "Maybe he talks with an accent. That ring a bell?"

Roman thought a moment, then said, "No, not right off."

"Mind if I take a turn around town?"

"How long you planning to stay?"

"How big is this town?" Decker asked. "How long does one turn take?"

"Be my guest," Roman said. "If you find him, though, I want to know about it."

"You will," Decker promised, putting the coffee cup down on the desk, "just as soon as I bring him in."

"Alive?"

Decker turned and said, "You know, you make a lousy cup of coffee."

Decker walked around town, wondering what he was looking for. Did he expect to find a man with a Russian accent twirling a gun or shooting the eyes out of flies? In order to find out if anyone had an accent, he'd have to talk to every man in town. He wasn't prepared to do that, not here and not in any other town he came to.

And what about other towns? Broadus was the first decent-sized town that he'd come to. Were there others farther along the river?

Decker decided to see about Broadus's two saloons.

One was called the Broadus House, the other the Dice Box. He guessed that the difference between the two was that the Dice Box would offer more gambling. He decided to try the Broadus House first.

Going to the bar, he ordered a beer. Surprised to find it a cold one, he downed half of it while the bartender watched, an amused look on his face.

"Been a while, huh?" the man said.

"Been a long while since I had one as cold as this," Decker admitted.

"Got our own ice house."

Finishing the beer, Decker said, "How about another one?"

"Sure."

The second one was cold, too, but nothing ever seems quite as cold or good as the first one. He decided to take his time with this one.

"Passing through?" the bartender asked.

"Yeah. Riding along the river for a while. This is the first town of any size that I've come to."

"Only one like it along the Powder River."

"Really?"

"Yep. Got to go east or west of here to get to another town. Up north you've got to go where the Tongue River meets the Yellowstone. That's about twenty-five miles west of the Powder."

"What town is that?"

"Miles City. If you keep following the Powder until it joins the Yellowstone, you'll be about six miles from Terry."

"And between here and there?"

"Keep riding north and the Powder takes a bend to the east. From the point of that bend it's about twenty miles to Ekalaka. I guess if you stick to the river, those are the three towns within reach."

"They all have telegraph offices?"

"I'd say yes, though I don't know for sure."

The bartender moved down the bar to take care of another customer, and Decker thought over what he had just learned.

If the Baron was indeed holing up near the river, Decker's guess was that he'd stay in Broadus or one of the towns the bartender had mentioned. If Decker rode directly from here to Terry, it would take him the better part of two days. If he stopped in between to go to those other towns, he'd end up with more than a week's worth of riding to do. If the Baron was not in any of those towns, Decker would have to ride south and start checking small settlements and shantytowns like Brenner's Fork.

Of course, he could use the telegraph lines to check those larger towns, but he'd have to find a co-operative lawman at the other end. As a rule, lawmen didn't like bounty hunters, so he knew he couldn't count on that.

It was worth a try, though.

"Another?" the bartender asked.

"Maybe later. What do you have in the way of gambling?"

"You might pick up a poker game here, but if you want green felt you got to go to the Dice Box. They got poker, blackjack, faro, roulette, and dice."

"Where's the telegraph office?"

"Out the front and two blocks to the right."

"Okay, thanks."

"Sure."

Decker left and headed for the telegraph

office, already composing his messages in his head.

After Decker had left the sheriff's office Kyle Roman thoughtfully poured himself another cup of coffee and drank it slowly.

He'd always wondered about Broadus's mystery man, the man who called himself Brand. The man who had come to town and destroyed his relationship with Josephine Hale. Josephine had been immediately taken with Brand, and instead of accepting it gracefully, Roman had reacted badly. The result had been that Josephine rarely spoke to him, even to say good morning on the street. Had he reacted differently, he might have won her back during one of Brand's absences, he knew, but it was far too late for that now.

He'd always wondered what the man did when he was away from Broadus, and he'd always wondered about the slow, precise manner in which the man spoke, as if he were trying to hide some sort of accent.

Now he knew.

Brand was the Baron.

With careful planning, that knowledge could be turned to a great advantage.

After Decker had sent his three carefully

worded telegraph messages to Miles City, Terry, and Ekalaka, he decided to take a look at the Dice House. They had gambling, but was their beer as cold as the beer at the Broadus House?

CHAPTER SEVENTEEN

As Sheriff Roman approached Josephine Hale's house he saw Brand sitting on the porch.

"Good afternoon, Brand," Roman said, putting his foot on the bottom step.

"Sheriff," Brand said, staring coldly at the man. Looking into those eyes now, Roman could see where the man could be a killer. "What can I do for you?"

"I thought we'd have a little talk."

"About what?"

"About you."

"What about me?"

Yes, Roman thought, now that he stopped to listen for it, he noticed a definite accent there. The man spoke as few words as possible, but he definitely had a slight accent.

"Well, I've always wondered where you went and what you did when you left Broadus, and now I think I've found out."

"Really?"

"Yes, really. Are you interested?"

"No."

"Well, I'm gonna tell you anyway," Roman said, milking the moment. "You kill people."

Brand did not react. He simply stared at Roman until the man began to fidget uncomfortably.

"Do I?"

"Oh yes, you do, for money — and you are known as the Baron."

"Where," Brand said, "did you get such an idea?"

"Oh, that I'm not at liberty to say. Let's just say that there's a man on his way here who would love for me to point my finger at you."

"And will you?"

"Well, I might."

Again there was a long period of silence, as if Brand was waiting for Roman to explain and Roman was waiting for Brand to ask.

Finally, it was Roman who impatiently broke the silence.

"Of course, I could be persuaded to keep my mouth shut."

"Oh? How?"

"Well, I'm sure for as long as you've been, um, in business you've probably put away a decent amount of money — maybe even in our bank."

Brand did not respond.

"Okay, look, I'm gonna give you some time to think this over," Roman said, taking his foot off the step, "but don't take too long. I might get impatient."

Roman hesitated, waiting to see if Brand had anything to say, and when nothing was forthcoming he turned and walked away. His back itched, even though he knew Brand was not wearing a gun.

Brand watched the lawman walk away and wondered what had happened. How had the man found out who he was? Was there really someone on the way — a lawman? a bounty hunter? — who was looking for him, or was that a lie?

Or worse, was that man already here?

He thought back to that job where he had accidentally killed the boy. Surely a poster would have been issued on him as a result of that incident.

Who, he wondered, would dare try to collect the bounty on a man with his reputation?

He knew of a lot of lawmen who would track him because it was their job, but there were only a few men he could think of who would track him for money.

The most prominent of those was a man called Decker. Brand knew the man's reputation. He even knew what kind of gun Decker wore, and he knew about the hangman's noose he carried on his saddle.

If Decker was here, then his world in Broadus was very close to coming apart.

Brand stood up and went into the house. Entering the bedroom he shared with Josephine, he opened a closet and reached all the way in the back on the floor. He took out something bulky that was wrapped in cloth and then slowly unwrapped it. Removing the gun from the holster, he inspected it.

It would have to be cleaned.

He always cleaned his gun just before he used it.

Josephine was surprised not to find Brand waiting for her on the porch, as he usually was. She entered the house and, not seeing him in the parlor or kitchen, went upstairs to the bedroom. She found him in front of the closet and was about to say something when she saw what was in his hand.

"Are you leaving again?" she asked, suddenly frightened.

He turned, surprised by her presence. The gun in his hand automatically pointed at her, and he abruptly turned it away.

"No, no," he said. "I'm not leaving . . ."

She entered the room.

"Then why do you have your gun? You don't usually take it out unless you're leaving."

"Jo —"

"Is something wrong?" she asked. "Is that it?"

"There *might* be a problem," he said, "but nothing for you to worry about."

"If it concerns you, then it's something for me to worry about," she said earnestly. She put her hands on his chest and said, "Brand, I never ask you what you do when you leave, but if you're in trouble, I want to help."

He tucked the gun into his belt and took her hands in his. "Let's sit down," he said, guiding her to the bed.

"Jo," he began, "in some parts of the country I'm considered something of . . . of an outlaw . . ."

CHAPTER EIGHTEEN

The beer at the Dice Box was not as cold as the beer at the Broadus House, but there certainly was enough gambling to satisfy a gambling man. Decker wasn't really a gambling man, but he enjoyed a good poker game as much as anyone.

It was getting on into evening now, and another thing the Dice Box had this time of day was women. They were young, attractive, and dressed in low-cut, sequined gowns. Decker decided to stay around for a while and then go back to the Broadus House, which was more his kind of place.

He took his beer and walked around, watching some of the gambling tables, listening to the conversations. It was possible that he might hear something helpful.

At one point one of the girls came over and leaned on his shoulder.

"Can I get you something, honey?" she asked, tracing the outline of his jaw with a long, painted nail.

She was young, very pretty and had a very deep, creamy cleavage, but she was wearing so much perfume that his head hurt and his nostrils burned.

"No, thanks," he said. "Why don't you check with one of the players?"

"Maybe later?" she asked.

"Maybe," he said, promising nothing.

She sashayed off and talked to some of the men who were playing blackjack, and it looked to Decker like she was having more luck with them than she'd had with him.

He was returning to the bar for another beer when he saw Sheriff Roman walk through the batwing doors. He stood at the bar, waiting to see what the lawman was going to do. In a few seconds Roman spotted him and came over to him.

"Evening, Decker."

"Sheriff," the bounty hunter said. "Making your rounds?"

"Huh? Oh, yeah, my rounds. Hey, Ernie, give me a beer, huh?" the sheriff said to the bartender. To Decker he said, "Interested in gambling?"

"Not really. I play a little poker now and then."

"Some pretty women working here."

"Sure are, but this really isn't my kind of place."

"Oh? What is?"

"The Broadus House. It seems a little simpler, much more my style."

"This place usually gets most of the action."

"That's why I'm still here."

"Hoping to hear something about this man you're looking for?"

"You never know," Decker said. "You haven't heard anything, have you, Sheriff?"

"Me? No, not a word," he said. "Oh, but I did hear something about you sending telegraph messages ahead to some of the other towns."

The only way he could have heard about that was to check with the telegraph office. Why would he have done that? Decker wondered.

"What's that all about?" Roman asked. "Trying to get the local law to do your job for you?"

"Just asking for some co-operation, is all. It could save me some time in the saddle."

"You don't really expect to get any help from real lawmen, do you?"

"Why not? You've been pretty co-operative, haven't you?"

"Sure I have," Roman laughed, "but I'm a

helluva guy."

"I've noticed."

"Does this mean you'll be staying in Broadus a little longer?"

"At least until I get some replies."

"I see."

Roman finished his beer and set the empty mug down on the bar.

"Well, I'd better, uh, continue my rounds. See you around, Decker."

"Sure, Sheriff. See you around."

Decker watched the man walk out, wondering what he had really come in for.

When Brand finished his story, Josephine stared at him for a few moments, as if she simply couldn't comprehend what he'd told her.

"Who is this man?" she finally asked.

"I can't be sure," he said. "It might be a bounty hunter named Decker."

"This Decker, is he dangerous?"

"He's the most dangerous bounty hunter there is," Brand admitted.

"Is there a way to find out if it's him?"

"There are two ways," he said. "One, we can check the livery. If there's a hangman's noose with his saddle, then it's him."

"A hangman's noose?"

"He carries it with him."

"That's horrible!" Josephine whispered, her eyes growing wider.

"I guess it's his lucky charm."

"Does he — does he use it?"

"Well, his bounty is usually collectable dead or alive."

"What's the other way to find out?"

"His gun. He wears a cut-down shotgun in a special holster. You can't miss it."

"I want to help," she said. "What do you want me to do?"

"All right," Brand said, "now listen closely . . ."

CHAPTER NINETEEN

About a half an hour after the sheriff left, Decker decided he'd had enough of the nonstop activity in the Dice Box. He went outside, crossing the street to go to the Broadus House.

The shot creased him on the top of the left shoulder, leaving him with a stinging pain. Throwing himself forward, he rolled for cover and came up with his gun out. As he checked the rooftops across the street, straining to see any sign of movement, he guessed he had the darkness to thank for his life. Before whoever was after him could get off another shot, he was up and running back toward the Dice Box.

He moved along the sidewalk, alert in case whoever had shot at him had an accomplice on the other side of the street. Finally, he came to an alley and ran down it, trying to get behind the saloon. If he was lucky, he might catch his assailant coming down off the roof.

When he got to the back he stopped short. It was pitch-black. He flattened against the wall, waiting and listening.

When he heard something, it was from farther along behind the buildings. Cursing to himself, he took off running, realizing that his assailant had already made it down from the roof. He must have taken the one shot and decided not to risk any more.

Decker ran along behind the buildings until he came to another alley. He flattened against the wall again and eased into the alley, expecting to hear a shot. When he heard nothing he began to move forward with more purpose until finally he was out in the street again.

He heard somebody running toward him and spun around, his gun ready to fire.

"Whoa! Easy!" Sheriff Roman shouted, holding his empty hands out in front of him.

"Sheriff!" Decker said. He lowered his gun and took a deep breath. "Did you see anybody run out of this alley?"

"Nobody but you."

"He couldn't have been that far ahead of me," Decker said, complaining. "I heard him —"

"I heard the shot and came running, but since there was only one I couldn't be sure where it had come from." He squinted through the darkness and asked suddenly, "Hey, are you hit?"

Decker put his hand on his shoulder and it came away covered with blood.

"Just a nick."

"Better get the doc to take a look at it. Come on, I'll take you over."

Decker looked up and down the street, then holstered his gun and reluctantly agreed. Whoever had taken the shot at him was gone.

"Did you see him at all?" Roman asked as they began walking.

"I didn't see a thing," Decker said bitterly. "Not a blessed thing."

In the doctor's office, which was above the general store, Decker went over his story again for the sheriff while his shoulder was being patched.

"Dug a nice furrow," the doctor said, "but all in all I'd say you were damn lucky."

"I agree," Roman said. "Tell me again what happened," and Decker went into his story.

"Sounds like whoever it was was waiting for you to come and expected to hit you with the one shot, otherwise you might have caught them coming down from the roof."

"That's what I figure," Decker said. "They took the shot and immediately left the roof. If I had been a little quicker in reacting —"

"Can't blame yourself for that," Roman said. "How were you to know they weren't waiting to take another shot?"

"I guess you're right."

The doctor cleaned the wound, bandaged it, and then told Decker to put his shirt back on.

"What do I owe you, Doc?" Decker said.

The doctor named a figure, and the bounty hunter paid him.

"Going back to your hotel?" Roman asked.

"I think I'll go over to the Broadus House and see if their whiskey is as good as their beer."

"If I were you I'd hole up in my room for a while. Whoever it was might decide to make another try tonight."

"I hope they do," Decker said. "This time I'll be a little quicker."

CHAPTER TWENTY

The Broadus House wasn't even half full, and there was a lone poker game going on in one corner. There was one girl working, and although she was as pretty — or prettier — than the ones across the street, her dress was not as fancy. It was low-cut, but it was plain.

Decker went to the bar, and the bartender smiled, remembering him.

"Beer?" he asked.

"Whiskey first, then a beer."

The bartender poured him a shot.

"Been across the street?"

"Yep."

"Like it?"

Decker made a face and said, "It's too damn noisy."

"Got some good-looking women over there, though, don't they?"

Decker glanced at the woman at the end of the bar, who looked back.

"You don't seem to be doing so bad here," he said.

"Ah, that's Martha. They've tried to hire her at the Dice Box, but she's loyal."

"Really?"

"She doesn't like the owners. They treat the women who work for them like slaves."

"And you don't?"

"I treat a woman like a woman," the bartender said. He saw the look on Decker's face and said, "Don't get me wrong. That ain't what I mean. I don't tell Martha she's got to get ten guys a night into her room or anything like that. She wants to take a guy upstairs, that's her business. All I want her for down here is to have guys buy her drinks."

"Sounds like a nice arrangement. What does she drink?"

"Anything."

"Give her what she wants, on me," Decker said.

"Sure."

Decker eyed Martha, who was young and blonde . . . and alive, just like he was — only he was *lucky* to be alive.

The bartender poured Martha a shot of whiskey. She raised the glass to Decker in thanks. Decker raised his in return, downed it, then called for his beer.

He took the beer over to the poker game and watched for a while. It was low stakes and slow-paced, and he had no desire to sit in.

"See that feller sitting on the porch at Jo's today?" one of them asked.

"Oh, yeah. Imagine living off a woman like that, jest sitting around her house while she works," another man said.

"What about the time he spends away?" someone asked. "Where do you suppose he goes?"

"Who knows?"

"Maybe he's got hisself a woman in another town," one of them said. "You know, like living two lives?"

Decker was listening intently.

"Unfriendly cuss, that one. You'd think since he's been in and out of this town nigh onto a year he'd say hello or something. He ever talk to you boys?"

"He's been in the store once or twice," one of them said. "Talks real slow and careful, like. Can't figure it out. Maybe he's simple-minded."

The others laughed at the prospect, although one of them said it was unlikely that a pretty woman like Josephine would take up with a simpleton.

Suddenly they looked up at Decker, as if

151

just realizing that he was watching.

"You wanna play, mister? We got an empty seat."

Decker turned and looked at Martha, who was standing at the bar. She smiled invitingly at him.

"Maybe just a little while," he said, taking the seat.

Or at least until he found out where this Josephine lived.

CHAPTER
TWENTY-ONE

Josephine was nervous, but she understood why Brand couldn't go to the livery stable himself and look at all the horses. If the man who was after him was in town, then he couldn't afford to be seen.

It was late, but the stable was still open. The liveryman, however, must have gone to have dinner. Josephine wondered why the man didn't lock up when he left the stable. It would be very easy for someone to steal a horse.

She entered the stable and found it shrouded in darkness. She looked around for a storm lamp, found one, and lit it. Carrying it with her, she went from stall to stall, hoping that she wouldn't find what she was looking for.

She found it, in a stall all the way in the back. The stall contained a good-looking gelding, and the saddle that went with the horse. Hanging from the saddlehorn was a hangman's noose.

She shivered when she saw it. She would have hugged herself except that she had the storm lamp in her hand. The gelding gave her a baleful stare, as if wondering who she was and what she was doing there. Then he looked away.

Josephine backed out of the stall hurriedly, then turned to run. As she did, her feet got tangled, and then the heel snapped off one of her shoes, causing her to fall. The storm lamp was jarred from her hand. It landed on a patch of hay, and she saw the flicker of flame as the hay started to catch fire. Moving quickly, she grabbed a nearby blanket and smothered the flame. Luckily, the oil had not leaked from the lantern or there would have been a blaze that she couldn't have put out with a blanket.

Moving as quickly as she could, Josephine put the lantern back on the wall hook where she had found it and ran out of the stable.

Brand waited at the house. He knew he should have gone to the stable himself, but he couldn't take the chance of being seen there. If Decker was in town, he was going to have to kill him, and it wouldn't do to be seen snooping around the man's horse.

Once he killed Decker, his only problem

would be the sheriff. He would be the only one who knew who Brand really was. He could pay the man for his silence, he thought. But once that started it would never stop.

No, he'd have to kill Roman, also, but in such a way that no one would suspect he had done it.

If he could kill both men quickly and without anyone finding out about it, there was a chance he could save his life here in Broadus.

He'd killed for less in the past.

No sooner had he started playing than Decker noticed something. One of the men at the table was a professional gambler. It struck him odd that such a man would be in a low-stakes game instead of across the street for much more money.

There was one glaring reason why he was over here.

He was cheating.

In the Broadus House, no one noticed, but across the street at the Dice Box he would have been caught almost immediately. So here he sat, stealing hard-earned money penny by penny instead of dollar by dollar — so to speak.

Decker was seated directly across from

the man, so he knew how the man was cheating.

The man — whom the others called "Cal" — was dealing now. He paused to cough, covering his mouth with a handkerchief from his jacket pocket.

"Excuse me," he said, replacing the handkerchief. "Cards are coming out, gentlemen. Draw poker."

He dealt each man five cards. Decker picked his up and spread them; he had three tens and thought this was as good a time as any to call the man for cheating. If the man seated to his left hadn't opened, he would have. Now, he raised.

"A dollar," he said, which was a large raise for this game. The others were losing, but they stayed in, possibly seeing the hand as a quick way to get some money back.

When the bet went around to Cal, he said, "I raise a dollar as well."

Since they all were in for the first dollar, they stayed for the second.

"Cards?"

"Two," said Decker when it was his turn.

When everyone had his cards, the opener timidly bet fifty cents.

"I raise," Decker said. "Two dollars."

The two players to his left folded, and Cal gave him a long look.

"Seems like you think you've got something, fella."

"Cost you money to find out."

"Oh, it'll cost one of us money," Cal said, "that's for sure. I raise ten dollars."

"Ten dollars?" the opener said. "That's . . . that's too high."

"Then fold," Cal said without looking at the man. "Leave this here game to me and mister. . . ."

Decker didn't bother supplying his name. He looked at the man who had opened, and the man quickly folded.

"I raise twenty," Decker said.

"Twenty?" Cal said. "This game is starting to sound like it belongs across the street."

At that point, Cal began coughing and took out his handkerchief. When he paused in his coughing he placed the handkerchief on the table, obstructing the view of his hand for a moment. He started coughing again, brought the cloth to his lips, and then replaced it in his pocket.

"I'll see you and raise you the same," he said to Decker.

Decker studied his cards for a moment, then said, "All right, I'll call. I've got three tens." He spread his cards on the table.

"Oh, too bad," Cal said. He put his cards

157

down, revealing an ace-high flush.

As he started to reach for the pot, Decker drew his gun and placed it on the table.

"If you touch that pot, I'll kill you."

Cal froze. He stared at Decker's face, then the shotgun, then his face again.

"I don't understand."

Everyone else in the place did, though. They crowded around to see who would get shot. They didn't much care which, as long as it was one of them. It would give them something to talk about.

"That isn't the hand I called," Decker said, indicating the cards on the table.

"What?"

"The hand I called is in your pocket," Decker said, "with your handkerchief."

"Are — are you accusing me of cheating?" Cal asked.

"Yes."

"For a small pot like this?"

"Yes."

Cal laughed nervously.

"If I was going to cheat, wouldn't it make more sense for me to work the Dice Box across the street? The games are bigger there."

"They'd also spot you in a minute there," Decker said, "like I did. You're not very good at it. Tell me, why is it your cough has suddenly cleared up?"

"My . . . cough?"

"Take out the handkerchief," Decker said.

Slowly, Cal sat back and reached into his pocket.

"If you come out with a gun, I'll kill you. If you come out with the handkerchief, and not the cards, I'll kill you. Have I made myself clear?"

Sweating, Cal nodded. He took the handkerchief out and placed it on the table. Decker leaned over and unfolded the cloth, revealing five playing cards, face down. He turned them over, showing everyone how they read.

"A pair of threes," Decker said. "That's the hand I called, and you lose."

Cal's hands were on the table, and he was nervously drumming his fingers.

Decker raked in his pot.

"Are — are you gonna — kill me?" Cal asked.

"For such a small pot?" Decker asked. "Certainly not — providing you're out of here in five minutes."

"I'm gone, mister." Cal pushed his chair back so quickly that it toppled over when he stood up. "I'm gone."

Decker watched the man run for the door, and the spectators went back to their drinking, disappointed that no one had been shot.

"We owe you, mister," one of the men at the table said.

"Just be careful who you play with in the future," Decker said, standing up.

"You ain't playing no more?" one of them asked.

Decker looked at the end of the bar, where Martha was still standing. "No, I have another appointment."

Chapter
Twenty-Two

Decker could count on the fingers of one hand the times in his life that he'd been with a whore. Most of them had taken place when he'd been much younger. In recent years, when he'd been with a woman, it was always by mutual choice; money had had nothing to do with it.

Martha was an exceptional whore. She was extremely lovely, with blonde hair, a slim waist, rounded hips, and full, shapely thighs. She was only about twenty-two and as close to being truly beautiful as any woman Decker had ever seen.

When she had taken a slightly drunk Decker to her room the night before, she had made him feel as if she were doing it out of desire. Through the night, when they'd made love, she'd made him feel as if he was the only man who had ever pleasured her like that.

When the bounty hunter woke up the next

morning he felt embarrassed and glad that Martha was still asleep. He rose, dressed, and put some money on her dresser before leaving. He looked at her while she slept, and she seemed even prettier than she'd been the night before, when her face had been all painted. Now it was clean, and he could see what she really looked like. He was sorry she was a whore and that they hadn't spent the night together just because they'd wanted to.

He knew why he'd gone with her. It had been a reaction to almost being killed. The worst way for a man to die was to be shot in the back, and he hadn't escaped by much last night. The best way for a man to know he was alive was to be with a woman — especially a woman as desirable and skilled in lovemaking as Martha.

Out on the street he stretched until his bones cracked. His eyes felt gritty because he'd only slept half the night, and his head ached from the whiskey he'd consumed hours before, but all in all he felt fine.

He was alive.

From his office Kyle Roman could see the Broadus House, and he happened to be looking out the window when Decker came out. Roman knew he couldn't very well put the squeeze on Brand if Decker took him in. He was going to have to find a way to deal with Decker.

He watched until the bounty hunter was out of sight. Then he walked away from the window and poured himself another cup of coffee.

The only reason a man would be coming out of that place early in the morning would be Martha. For a moment the sheriff envied Decker. He'd spent some time with Martha himself.

The next moment, Roman smiled as he figured out a way to get Decker out of his way without killing him.

Decker entered the livery stable to check on John Henry and found the liveryman in an agitated state, mumbling to himself and shaking his head.

"What's wrong?" Decker asked.

"Looks like there was a fire here last night," the old man said.

"A fire?" Decker demanded. "Is my horse all right?"

"Oh, sure, mister. Your horse is fine. Fact of the matter is, it was just a small fire. Looks like somebody put it out with a blanket."

"Where was the fire?"

"Come to think of it, it was in front of your horse's stall."

"Show me."

The old man led Decker to the spot, and sure enough, there was a scorched patch of hay just across from John Henry's stall. He went into the stall to check the horse.

"How you doing, boy?" he said. The gelding turned his head and looked at Decker. "Had some excitement here last night? Huh?"

He patted the gelding's neck, checked him to make sure he hadn't been injured, and then left the stall. As he did, he stepped on something and looked down.

"What's this?" he asked.

"What?" the old man said.

Decker bent over and picked the object up. "It's the heel of a shoe."

"Looks like it's from a woman's shoe."

"Yeah," Decker said, turning it over in his hand. "Doesn't it?"

He looked down at the burnt hay and the scorched blanket. Then he thought about what the man at the poker table had said the night before, about Josephine and her strange man. During the course of the game one of the men had mentioned that the house was at the south end of town.

He wondered if Miss Josephine wasn't

missing a heel from her shoe today. Decker found a café that was open early and went inside for breakfast. He was glad to be the only customer and put the shoe heel on the table while he ate his eggs and bacon.

If the man living with Josephine was the Baron, then why would he have sent her to the livery? What would she have been doing near John Henry's stall?

What would she have seen while she was there?

A horse . . .

A saddle . . .

And then it hit him.

The hangman's noose.

His trademark.

Now the Baron knew that Decker was there, but how had he known to send someone to the livery to look? And how had he become aware that Decker was after him in the first place? There was only one answer to that.

Sheriff Kyle Roman.

For some reason, Roman had gone to the Baron and told him that Decker was in town — no, if he had mentioned Decker by name, then the Baron wouldn't have sent his woman to the livery to check.

Roman was playing his own game here but what was it? If he and the Baron were friends, then he surely would have mentioned Decker by name. Why hadn't he?

Decker was drinking a cup of coffee when Roman walked into the café. He spotted Decker and walked right over to his table.

"Decker," he said, "I got to take you in."

"For what?" the bounty hunter demanded.

"Murder."

Decker stared at the man and said, "What the hell are you talking about?"

"You were with a girl named Martha last night."

"So?"

"So this morning she's dead, strangled."

"What?"

"I'm arresting you for her murder."

CHAPTER
TWENTY-THREE

The instant Roman looked into Decker's cold eyes he knew he'd made a terrible mistake. He went for his gun but Decker said, "Don't do it, Sheriff."

Roman froze.

"I've got my gun on you under the table. It's been pointing at you since you walked in."

Roman wet his lips and then said, "You're bluffing."

"Try me," Decker said. "You've seen my gun. It won't be any problem for me to fire through this table."

Again, Roman wet his lips.

"You can't do this, Decker. I'm the law here."

"Piss-poor excuse for a lawman, if you ask me. What kind of evidence do you have against me to arrest me?"

"You were the last one with her."

"She was alive when I left."

"You can't prove that."

"And you can't prove she wasn't."

"That's for a jury to decide."

"No," Decker said, shaking his head. "What's your game, Roman? You want me out of the way so you can deal with the Baron? You can't collect the bounty. As a matter of fact, I doubt you're man enough to even try him."

Roman didn't answer. He was standing there very awkwardly, beginning to sweat, not knowing what to do.

"Oh, wait a minute, I get it now," Decker said. "Blackmail. You and I are the only ones who know who he really is. Get me out of the way and you can make him pay for your silence, huh?"

"I don't know what you're talking about."

"He won't pay you, you know," Decker said. "He'll just kill you."

Roman frowned, wetting his lips again.

"My breakfast is getting cold, Sheriff," Decker said. "I'd appreciate it if you would get out of here and let me finish."

"I'll just wait for you outside and arrest you there, Decker."

"No, you won't. If you try me, Roman, I'll kill you."

"You can't kill a town sheriff. You'd be on the run for the rest of your life."

"That won't concern you, because you'll be dead. Think about that."

When the sheriff didn't move Decker took his sawed-off out from beneath the table just to show the lawman that he wasn't bluffing.

"Jesus —" Roman muttered, staring at the shotgun. Then he slowly backed out of the café.

Decker holstered his gun and continued with his breakfast.

He was at odds now with the town sheriff, and that was not good at all.

He felt bad about Martha and figured that either the Baron killed her to frame him, or the sheriff himself did it. His money was on the sheriff. Roman didn't have the nerve to try to kill Decker, but strangling a woman and pinning it on him was easier. He didn't think a man like the Baron would have murdered a woman. If he wanted Decker out of the way, he'd face him and try to kill him himself.

Decker's shoulder twitched, and he suddenly realized that it must have been Sheriff Roman who'd taken the shot at him the night before. That made him wish the man *had* drawn on him.

Furious, Kyle Roman stalked back to his

office. He had let Decker back him down and he hated himself for it. He also cursed himself for missing the man the night before. He should have taken the time to get himself a rifle and not tried to make the shot with a handgun.

In his office he slammed his door, kicked his desk, and threw himself into his chair. He looked at his hands, which were still shaking. Decker was crazy to threaten a lawman. In fact, the man was just plain crazy, he thought.

Kyle clenched his fists and wished he'd had the nerve to wait for Decker to come out of the café and arrest the bounty hunter then.

Shit! he thought, he'd sneaked up to Martha's room and strangled her in her sleep for nothing. There was no way he could prove to anyone — least of all a federal judge — that Decker had killed the girl, and Roman didn't want a judge in town while Decker could possibly point a finger at him.

Decker had to die, and if Roman couldn't do the job himself, he knew someone who could.

Decker finished his breakfast and readied himself to go out into the street. He didn't like the feeling of being on the wrong side of the law, but then he didn't consider Sheriff Roman to be much of a sheriff. The man was obviously out for himself, so it wouldn't bother Decker to have to kill Roman if he got in his way. He'd have to square himself with the federal law on that, but he thought he could.

All he had to do was prove that Roman was using his badge to blackmail a wanted killer — and that he murdered an innocent woman as a means to further his own ends.

Decker stepped out on the boardwalk and looked around. He couldn't see Roman anywhere, but if last night was any indication, the man was quite capable of back-shooting him. The only thing that might have kept him from doing that now was the fact that it was broad daylight.

Decker was really going to have to watch his step once darkness fell.

CHAPTER
TWENTY-FOUR

Decker walked to the telegraph office to see if he'd received any replies to his wires. Fairly sure now that the Baron was in Broadus, he didn't really think the wires were important any longer, but if he had received any co-operation from the lawmen in the other towns, he wanted to be able to acknowledge them.

As it turned out, he received no offers of co-operation. Apparently the lawmen in all three towns had no liking for bounty hunters, for none of them offered him the slightest bit of help.

It was just as well.

He tore up the messages and discarded them, then stepped outside.

Over breakfast Josephine asked Brand, "What are we going to do?"

"About what?"

"About what?" she asked. "About that

man Decker."

Brand looked at her across the table. She had come home in a highly agitated state the night before and had not been able to sleep very well. She looked drawn and haggard.

"Don't worry about it," Brand said.

"How can I not worry about it?"

"Go to work."

She looked at him as if he were crazy.

"I can't go to work!" she said.

"Sure you can."

"Lucy can run the shop," she told him, referring to the woman who worked for her.

"I want you to go to work, Josephine," Brand said softly. "I don't want to have to worry about you. Worrying about you could get me killed."

"I don't —" Josephine said, and then she stopped. She had been about to say that she didn't understand that, but suddenly she did.

"All right," she said. "I'll go to work."

"Good girl."

"What are you going to do?"

"I think," Brand said, "I'll have a talk with our new friend, Decker."

"You're going to talk to the man who wants to kill you?" she asked incredulously.

"Maybe he can be reasoned with."

"If everything you've said about him is true, I don't see how you can hope to —"

"Sometimes," he said, "I can be very persuasive."

Kyle Roman was standing across the street from Josephine Hale's house, waiting for her to go to work. For a while it looked as if she wasn't going to leave, but finally the front door opened and she stepped out. He waited until she was out of sight before he crossed the street and knocked on the front door.

After a few moments the man known in Broadus as Brand, now known to Roman as the Baron, answered the door.

"What do you want?" he asked.

"We have to talk."

"About what?"

"About a man called Decker," Roman said, looking as if he expected the name to mean something to Brand.

"I know all about Decker."

That deflated Roman for the moment.

"You do?"

"Yes."

"Well . . . what are we going to do about him?"

"What are *we* going to do?" Brand asked.

"That's right."

"Have you had breakfast yet, Sheriff?"

"No," Roman said, looking confused.

"Well, come in and have a cup of coffee."

At the poker game the night before Decker had not only found out where Josephine Hale lived, but also where she worked. He was standing across the street from her shop when she opened the front door with a key and entered. Only then did he step out of the doorway and start toward the southern end of town. Roman had two cups of coffee and listened to what Brand had to say.

"You want me to stay out of it?" he asked when Brand was finished.

"That's right," Brand said. "Decker is my problem, not yours."

"But —"

"But what?"

"I — I —"

"Wait a minute," Brand said. "I heard something about a shooting last night. That wasn't you, was it?"

Roman stared helplessly at Brand.

"Did you try to shoot him in the back?" Brand asked.

"What are you getting so upset about?" Roman demanded. "If I'd killed him, you wouldn't have to worry about him."

"You son of a bitch!" Brand said. He

reached across the table and pulled Roman to him by the shirt front. "I've never shot a man in the back in my life. Are you that much of a spineless coward?"

"I — I —"

Brand released Roman and pushed him back into his chair, where the man sat and stared at him, bewildered.

Brand stood up and began to walk around the table.

"What else have you pulled?" Brand asked. "Tell me."

"Well —"

"Come on!" Brand shouted, poking Roman in the arm, jarring him. "Tell me."

"I . . . I tried to frame him for murder."

"Well, that was smart. How did that work?"

"It didn't."

"Tell me about it. Come on, if we're going to be partners in this, you have to tell me everything."

Reluctantly, Roman told Brand what he had done to Martha after Decker had left her. Brand listened, continuing to circle the table.

"So, you killed an innocent woman for nothing."

"Well, you — you killed an innocent boy,

176

didn't you? Isn't that why Decker's after you?"

"That was an accident," Brand said, "an unfortunate accident. You, my friend, cold-bloodedly killed a woman who had nothing whatsoever to do with all of this."

"It was the only thing I could think of."

"And this," Brand said, stopping behind Sheriff Kyle Roman, "is all I can think of."

Too swiftly for the sheriff to realize what was happening, Brand slid his left forearm around Roman's neck, put his right hand beneath the man's chin, and twisted viciously. Roman's body stiffened, shivered, and then went limp.

"That's one problem solved," Brand said, straightening up.

Decker stood across the street from Josephine's house, trying to decide what to do. Finally he crossed the street and moved alongside the house, stealthily peering into windows as he went. When he finally got to the kitchen window he stopped and watched as a man stood behind the sheriff and quickly and efficiently broke his neck. There was no question about it. Only a man like the Baron would be capable of such an act. The bounty hunter had found his quarry at last.

Decker couldn't really feel sorry for the sheriff. He had obviously gotten in way over his head due to greed.

Decker watched a moment longer, assessing his foe. The Baron lifted Roman up and tossed him over his shoulder. The man was obviously very strong, evidenced by both the move he'd used to break the man's neck and the ease with which he was carrying the now-dead weight.

Rather than stay and watch the Baron dispose of the body, Decker decided to go somewhere to think and decide how best to confront this formidable opponent.

CHAPTER TWENTY-FIVE

Decker decided to go to the Broadus House and talk to the bartender, whose name he didn't remember — if he'd ever known it at all. He wanted to assure the man that he had had nothing to do with Martha's death.

When he reached the saloon the doors were locked, and he banged on them until they were opened.

"Decker," the bartender said.

"Can I come in?"

"Sure."

The man stepped back and allowed the bounty hunter to enter.

"I heard what happened to Martha," Decker said. "I'm sorry."

"So am I."

"Where is she?"

"The undertaker's."

"Was the sheriff here?"

"He sure was."

"He interrupted my breakfast by trying to

arrest me for her murder."

"That's crazy," the man said.

"Why do you say that? He seemed to think that since I was the last one with her, I was the logical suspect. In fact, I was afraid you'd believe it, too."

"Naw," the man said. "I saw Martha after you left her."

"You did?"

He nodded.

"And she was fine. We exchanged a few words and then she went back to bed. Next thing I knew, she was dead."

"I think I know who killed her."

The bartender's eyes widened and he asked, "Who?"

"The sheriff."

"What?"

Decker explained his reasoning, and the bartender listened, nodding.

"The poor kid," he said when Decker was finished. "If what you say is true, then she died for something she wasn't even involved in."

"I'm afraid so."

"Shit!" the man said.

"I don't think I ever even learned your name," Decker said.

"Potts."

"Well, Mr. Potts, I'm sorry."

"Not your fault. I'd like to see that sheriff get his, though."

"Don't worry," Decker said, opening the door to leave. "I'm sure he will."

As he walked down the street, Decker got an idea and headed for the store that Josephine ran. As he entered, a little bell above the door tinkled, announcing his presence. The woman behind the counter looked up and smiled at him.

"May I help you, sir?" the woman asked. "Something for your wife?"

"I'd like to see the owner," Decker said. "Miss Hale."

"I can help you just as well —" the young woman began, but Decker cut her off.

"I'm sure you can, and I mean no disrespect, but I'd rather see Miss Hale."

"Very well," the woman said. "If you'll wait one moment?"

"Of course."

The woman disappeared through a curtained doorway, and when the curtain parted again Josephine Hale came through. Decker was surprised at how tall she was, her eyes nearly level with his.

"Yes? Can I help you?" she asked.

"Maybe I can help you," Decker told her.

"Oh? How?"

Decker took the shoe heel he'd found in

the livery from his pocket and laid it on the counter.

"You lost that."

She looked at the heel, her eyes widening. Then she looked at Decker and saw the distinctive gun on his hip.

"Decker!" she said, her voice a harsh whisper.

"That's right."

She tried to run, but he grabbed her by the wrist.

"Please," he said, holding her tightly. "I'm not here to frighten you or hurt you."

"You *are* hurting me," she said, trying to pull free.

"I'm sorry. When I let you go, please don't try to run. We have to talk."

"I'll call the sheriff," she said defiantly.

"I doubt he'll be able to come. Your man broke his neck this morning."

She stopped struggling and simply stared at him, a look of horror on her face.

He released her wrist, but she didn't seem to notice.

"He broke his neck, right in your kitchen."

She slapped him then, hard enough to make his ears ring.

"You're a liar!"

"I'm not," Decker said. "What name does he go by, this man of yours."

"You know his name. You're hunting him!" she snapped.

"I know him as the Baron," Decker said, "but I don't know his real name."

"The Baron?" she asked, confused. "His name is Brand."

"Just Brand?"

"It — it's all I know."

"He lives with you, and that's all you know?"

"That's all . . . he ever told me."

"I'm sorry to show you this, Miss Hale," he said, taking the poster from his pocket and handing it to her.

She read it, a growing look of horror on her face.

"A — a professional killer?" she said, staring at Decker. He winced at the pain he saw in her eyes but consoled himself with the knowledge that he wasn't causing the pain, her man was.

"Yes."

"It can't be."

He took the poster from her.

"What did he tell you?"

"That he had been framed for killing someone and that you were a bounty hunter. He said you wouldn't be concerned with whether or not he was guilty, you'd just want to take him in."

"He's right," Decker said. "As far as it goes, that's all true. I hunt men for bounty and bring them in for trial. It's up to a judge and jury to decide if they're guilty or not. As a matter of fact, most of the men I hunt have already been found guilty."

"But not . . . him?"

"Not yet. He'll have to stand trial."

"He — he said you'd want to kill him."

"That's why I came to see you," Decker said. "Go to him, tell him I don't want to kill him. Convince him to come back with me."

"I can't —" she said, tears streaming down her face. "I can't . . . go back there —"

"Whatever he's done, Miss Hale," Decker said, "I'm sure he loves you, or else why would he have kept coming back?"

"You're — you're confusing me," she said. "First you say he's a killer, then you say he loves me."

"One doesn't prevent the other from being true."

"It can't — that can't be true. How could such a man — love?"

"Believe me," Decker said, "all men can love, no matter what they do for a living."

She looked at him now as if seeing him for the first time.

"You're a strange man."

184

"No stranger than he, or any other man. I've got a job to do, and I'd rather do it without killing him."

"But — but you will if you have to."

"If he forces me to," Decker said, "yes."

"Or he may kill you."

"That's very possible."

"And yet you'll still try to bring him in?"

"Yes."

"To — to bring him to justice?"

"Please, don't try to make me out some sort of saint, ma'am," Decker said. "I want to bring him in for the bounty. No other reason."

"I don't —" she said, shaking her head, "I don't understand either one of you."

"I'm not asking you to understand us, I'm asking you to save one of us from being killed and one of us from killing."

"I don't — I still can't believe —"

"Go and talk to him. You'll know when he's telling you the truth."

"Yes," she murmured, "yes . . ." She looked at him and asked, "Where will you be?"

He thought a moment, then said, "The Broadus House."

She nodded and told him, "I have to go home."

"I'm sorry about what I have to do. I truly am."

She looked at his face again and said, "Yes, I do believe you are."

CHAPTER TWENTY-SIX

Brand had just finished disposing of Sheriff Roman's body — albeit temporarily — when he heard the front door of the house open. He stiffened, then relaxed when Josephine came into the kitchen.

"What are you doing home?" he asked. Then he saw her face and said, "What the hell is wrong?"

"He came to see me."

"Who?"

"Decker."

"He did? What did he want?"

"He wants me to tell you that he doesn't want to kill you."

"That's what he said?"

"Yes."

He studied her for a moment and then asked, "And you believed him?"

"Yes," she admitted, lifting her chin, "I did."

Brand frowned and asked, "What else did

he tell you?"

"That you were a professional killer called the Baron, and then he showed me a wanted poster." There was a long pause, but she finally asked, "Is that what you were doing all those times you were gone? Killing people?"

"I was doing," he said, "what I have to do to survive."

"You have to kill to survive?"

"We all have to kill to survive, Josephine," he said. "Sometimes."

"I can't believe that."

"But you believed everything that Decker told you."

"Yes."

"Why?"

"Because he didn't try to lie about what he is. He said that everything you told me about him was true. Tell me, Brand, if he has no need to lie about himself, why would he have to lie about you?"

Brand was about to protest when he saw that it would do no good. Josephine finally knew who he was, and what he was.

"Josephine —"

"He also said you killed the sheriff in this room, broke his neck. Is that true?"

Jesus! Brand thought. Had Decker seen that? How was that possible?

"Yes."

"Why?"

"He didn't deserve to live. He was trying to blackmail me. He tried to shoot Decker in the back, and he killed a whore to try and blame Decker for it."

"Then he was no different from you or Decker. You're all killers."

"Yes."

"My God —" she moaned. She started to sit at the kitchen table and then suddenly stiffened and jumped away. "God! I can't even live here anymore."

"Josephine," he said. He moved to touch her but she flinched. "We can go somewhere else —"

"How can we?" she asked. "How can I forget what happened here? How can I forget the lies?"

"I never lied to you," he said. "I never told you what I did when I was away, and you never asked."

"No, you're right," she said. "I never asked. I'm just as much to blame for all of this as you are."

"Nobody's to blame —"

"He doesn't want to kill you," she said, "he just wants to take you back."

"So *they* can kill me," he replied bitterly. "Make me dance at the end of a rope."

"Please!" she said, clapping her hands to her ears.

"That's what they'll do to me, Jo. They'll hang me."

She removed her hands from her ears and said, "Only if you deserve it."

He stared at her then, knowing that he had finally lost her, as he'd always known he would someday.

"All right," he said dejectedly.

"You'll turn yourself over to him?"

"Where is he?"

"At the Broadus House."

"I'll go and see him."

"I'll go and tell him you're coming," she said.

"There's no need," he assured her. "He knows I'm coming."

"How?"

"Believe me," Brand said, "he knows."

When Brand left the house without his gun Josephine assumed that he was going to turn himself over to Decker.

She was wrong.

CHAPTER
TWENTY-SEVEN

Decker was surprised when the Baron walked into the saloon, which was empty except for him and the bartender. Potts had consented to open it, once Decker told him why.

Decker was surprised not only that the Baron walked boldly into the saloon, but also by the fact that he was unarmed.

The Baron — who, he now knew, was called Brand in Broadus, and, hell, maybe that was even his real name — walked right up to Decker's table.

"Decker?" he asked, his voice devoid of all emotion.

"That's right."

"I am Brand — or, as you know me, the Baron."

"Have a seat."

"You see that I am unarmed."

"I noticed."

Brand sat directly across from the

bounty hunter.

"You realize what that means?"

"You're here to talk."

"Yes, but lest you think you can hold me because I am unarmed —"

"You'd make me kill you."

"Exactly. You would have to be willing to shoot down an unarmed man in front of a witness," he said, inclining his head toward Potts, who was still behind the bar.

"You want me to leave?" Potts asked Decker.

"No need," Decker said. "All right, Brand, let's talk."

"I will not go back with you," Brand said quickly, "not alive."

"That doesn't leave a whole hell of a lot for me to say, does it?"

"I am asking you to leave Broadus and forget about me. I do not want to kill you."

"Nor I you, but there doesn't seem to be any other way — unless you want to change your mind and come with me willingly."

"I cannot do that. I would be submitting myself to a hangman's noose."

Decker knew what that was like and unconsciously touched his own neck where a noose had once rested.

Brand seemed to notice the move and narrowed his eyes as an idea struck him.

"That's why you carry that noose with you, isn't it?" he said suddenly. "You've had it around your neck, haven't you? Maybe you've even had *that* one around your neck."

Decker was surprised at the man's perception and was thrown off balance by it.

"I don't think we're here to discuss my past," he said lamely.

"Still, if that is your past, how can you justify bringing men in and subjecting them to the same —"

"I don't have to justify myself to anyone," Decker stated forcefully, "least of all to you."

Their eyes met, and for a few seconds, neither man said anything.

"Are you prepared to come with me willingly?" Decker finally asked, breaking the silence.

"No."

"Then you'd better get up and leave while you can. I'll be coming for you today — unless you run."

The man called the Baron laughed then.

"Do you think I'm afraid of you?" he asked.

"Yes," Decker said, "just as I am afraid of you. You'd be a fool not to be."

"Josephine was right about you," he said and rose. Decker did not ask him to explain the remark.

The bounty hunter watched the Baron leave the saloon, wondering if he shouldn't have tried to hold him while he had him. He might have been able to do it without killing him if he had played his cards just right.

Or maybe he wanted to kill him. Maybe what Brand had been saying about the noose and all was too close to being right on the money.

"You just let him walk out!" Potts said in amazement. "What if he runs?"

"He won't run." Decker looked at Potts and said, "Too early for a drink?"

"For me to serve or for you to drink?" Potts asked, but he poured it without waiting for an answer and took it to Decker's table.

When Brand got back to the house Josephine was not there. He assumed that she had gone back to the store. That was just as well, he thought. There was no point in trying to talk to her now. Might as well wait for this thing to be over before trying to patch things up with her.

He went up to the bedroom and pulled out his gun again. He had put it back after Josephine caught him with it. Now he pulled the big Colt .44 from his holster and began to clean it.

Decker sat in the saloon and worked on his drink. It was all over now but the shooting, and the when and where of that seemed to be up to him — that is, unless Brand chose to hole up in that house. Then Decker would have to go in and get him. Somehow, though, he didn't think that would be the Baron's style. If he died, he'd want to die on his feet, in the street, and if he killed Decker, he'd want it to be face to face.

As would Decker.

CHAPTER
TWENTY-EIGHT

Almost afraid to breathe, Josephine had stood in a doorway waiting for something to happen in the Broadus House across the street. When Brand finally came out and started down the street she realized that she had been holding her breath.

Her first thought was to run after Brand and go home with him, but he wasn't the same man she had known and loved for so long and home wasn't home anymore, either.

Once Brand was out of sight, she hurried across the street and into the saloon. Seeing Decker sitting alone at a table, she approached him.

Decker saw Josephine enter the saloon. Somehow her presence didn't surprise him.

When she sat across from him, he asked, "Would you like a cup of coffee?"

"Yes, please," she said in a whisper. He noticed that her hands were shaking.

"Potts!" Decker called. "Can we get some coffee?"

"Sure."

When Decker looked back at Josephine she was clasping her hands tightly together, as if she too had noticed that they were trembling and was trying to stop them.

"I saw him leave," she said. "Was — was anything resolved?"

"Yes," Decker said. "He said I won't take him alive."

She closed her eyes and bit her lip.

"I knew it," she said, her voice barely audible.

"Josephine —"

"No," she said, holding up her hand. "It's all right. It surprises me, but I think I understand."

Potts came over with a pot of coffee and two cups. Decker poured the coffee and pushed a cup across the table to her.

She looked at the cup but did not touch it.

"I — don't know where to go," she said finally. "I can't go back to — to that house. I can't go back to *him* . . . and yet I still love him."

"Of course you do," Decker said. "He hasn't done anything to you."

"But he has," she moaned. "He's ruined

197

everything between us."

"I ruined everything between you."

"No," she said. "If it hadn't been you who came after him, it would have been someone else. You can't take any blame for something he brought on himself."

Decker didn't reply to that. He sipped his coffee and waited for her to continue talking.

"I can't go back to work," she said. "I just can't face anyone —" She looked at him and said, "This will be resolved today, won't it?"

"Yes," he assured her. "One way or another, it will."

"When will you go after him?"

"I don't know."

"Didn't you, uh, agree . . ."

"You mean didn't we agree to meet in the street at a certain time?"

She nodded.

"It's not done that way, Josephine. No doubt he's gone back to your house to get his gun. He may wait for me there or he may come out. I might sit here for a while or I might go out into the streets. Sooner or later we'll be facing each other, and that's when it will happen."

"How — how can you stand — to wait?" she asked. "Either of you?"

He smiled.

"A man can always wait to die, Josephine."

"Are you prepared to die?"

He thought back to that day he'd stood on the gallows with a rope around his neck.

"I've been prepared to die for a long time."

"You amaze me."

"I shouldn't."

"Do you think I could stay here . . . until it's all over? I couldn't stand to see . . ."

"Potts!" Decker said.

Potts had been listening, and he said, "Sure. I could use the company."

Decker wished she would get up and leave, because if she stayed he would have to leave. He couldn't possibly sit there with her watching him.

"I don't know . . . what to do . . ." she said lamely.

"Just sit here," he told her, "and wait."

He stood up, pushing his chair back. As he started past her to the door, she grabbed his arm with both hands, a desperate look in her eyes.

"Don't —" she started, then her voice broke. Abruptly she turned away from him and said, "Be careful."

Decker was sure that was not what she had intended to say.

After Decker left, Potts walked over to the

table and asked Josephine, "Would you like me to heat this coffee up?"

For a moment he thought she hadn't heard him, and then she looked at him and said, "May I have a glass of whiskey, please?"

CHAPTER TWENTY-NINE

Decker sat in a straight-backed wooden chair in front of his hotel and cleaned his gun. When that was done he picked up his rifle and cleaned that as well. He had a clear view of the street and, with his back to the wall, there was no chance of anyone getting behind him.

It was the thought of Josephine sitting in the saloon that finally prompted him to rise, pick up his rifle, and start down the street toward her house.

Might as well get it over with and not make the poor woman wait, he thought. Brand wondered where Josephine was, then pushed all thoughts of the woman from his mind. He couldn't very well concentrate on Decker if he was thinking about her.

He strapped on his gun and checked his rifle one more time. He looked out the parlor window just in time to see Decker walking toward the house.

So this was it.

"Brand!" Decker called out when he stood directly in front of Josephine Hale's house. He couldn't even be sure if Brand was inside anymore.

"Brand! It's time to leave, Brand!"

Decker waited, wondering if he should go to the back door and try to get in. He doubted that Brand was going to come out and just face him in the street.

He was about to move when he heard glass breaking and saw the barrel of a rifle poke out the window.

"Decker!"

"I'm here."

"Come on in and get me, Decker. You don't think I'm coming out there, do you?"

"It would be a lot easier."

"Forget it," Brand said. There was a shot, and some dirt was kicked up at Decker's feet.

Decker knew that Brand had missed on purpose. He had simply fired to signify that this was it.

"I'm coming in," Decker said.

"Come ahead!"

Before Brand could fire again Decker ran to his right, out of sight behind a nearby building. From there he worked his way around behind the building, and then to the back of Josephine's house. He flattened himself against the wall and carefully made his way to the back door, first peering into the kitchen window.

Next to the back door was a wooden bin which was probably used for wood. Ducking low and moving as quickly as he could, Decker got to the bin and opened it.

As he suspected, the body of Kyle Roman had been squeezed inside. Brand must have had to break the corpse's legs to fit him in there, another testament to the man's strength.

Decker closed the bin, took a step back, and, holding his rifle chest-high, kicked the door with all his strength. Wood splintered, and the door crashed open. Decker went in quickly, holding the rifle out ahead of him. The kitchen was empty, and he flattened himself against a wall, listening intently, watching the door to the rest of the house.

For all he knew, Brand could have gone out the front door. Before he could verify that, he was going to have to check the whole house. If Brand wanted to run, he had plenty of time to go to the livery, saddle a horse, and get out.

Decker was counting on Brand's readiness to finish this here and now. He was certain the Baron was not the sort of man who'd run.

Sliding along the wall, he worked his way to the doorway and slowly peered around the corner. He found himself looking into the parlor. From his vantage point he could see the window that Brand had broken. The front door was still closed, so if Brand had left the house, he had closed the door behind him. If not, then he had most likely gone upstairs.

Decker eased into the parlor, his rifle ready, and checked behind the sofa. Confident that the room was empty — and, in fact, that the first floor was empty — he moved to the stairway. He listened intently, trying to hear some indication that Brand was upstairs. The scrape of a boot, the creak of a floorboard would have been welcome, but there was nothing.

Slowly, he started up the stairs, taking them one at a time, alert in case any of them creaked, giving *him* away.

Finally he reached the top step, sweat dripping from his chin. The inside of the house had become oppressively hot. His hands were slick on the metal of his rifle, and he wiped them on his pants one at a time.

At the top of the stairs he had to step around a corner in order to get a look at the second-floor corridor. Knowing that Brand would never fall for such a trick, he took off his hat anyway, hung it on the end of the rifle, and dangled it around the corner.

Nothing.

He put his hat back on, steeled himself, and then leaped into the corridor, staying low.

The corridor was empty.

There were apparently two rooms on this floor, one behind him and one in front of him. The room in the front would overlook the street.

Decker backed down the corridor to the room behind him, stopped just past the door and then repeated the technique he used to open the kitchen door. He hoped Josephine wouldn't be too upset about all the broken doors.

This room was empty. Not only was there no one in it, there was no furniture in it, either. There were some cartons on the floor, but none large enough to hide a man. It was obviously used as a storeroom.

That left the front room, which must be the bedroom.

He moved down the corridor to the door, listened for a few seconds, then kicked it open and ducked inside. He swiftly covered the room with his rifle, first left, then right, but there was no sign of anyone there. Quickly, feeling foolish, he checked under the bed and in the closet, then stood up straight. Brand had obviously left the room, but where had he gone?

Decker was about to leave when he saw something on the window. Moving closer, he realized that it was a piece of paper hanging from the window lock. He walked over to it, saw that it was a note, reached for it — then cursed and threw himself to the floor just as a shot shattered the window.

"Shit!" he said between his teeth.

He had almost allowed himself to be suckered into standing in front of the window.

Cautiously he moved to the window on his knees, avoiding the broken glass, and peered up over the window ledge. He was in time to see Brand retreating toward town.

Decker grabbed the note off the window and sat with his back to the wall to read it.

DECKER,
　MEET ME IN TOWN FOR A HOT TIME
　　　　　　　　　　　THE BARON

It was an invitation he couldn't refuse.

CHAPTER
THIRTY

Decker left the house knowing that Brand had turned this entire contest to his own advantage. He had waited for Decker to move inside the house, and then had left by the front door, closing it behind him. He probably hadn't expected that trick with the note to work any more than Decker had expected his trick with the hat on the end of the gun to work.

Now Brand had moved the battle to the streets of the town, where he would probably assume that Decker would be concerned with the welfare of innocent bystanders.

If Brand was not concerned, then he had obviously given up all chances of saving his life in Broadus.

Now he was only trying to save his life.

Brand was undecided.

Initially he'd wondered if he wouldn't be

foolish not to go to the livery, saddle up, and ride out, but he knew that all that would do was postpone this showdown between him and Decker. He knew Decker's reputation as a bulldog. He hunted one man until he caught him, no matter how long it took.

That kind of man would have to be taken care of now, when he had the chance.

Now he was undecided as to whether he should stay on street level or move to the rooftops. He had the whole town to play with, having effectively put Decker at a disadvantage.

It was then that he realized he was actually enjoying this.

With the whole town at his command, he was like a kid in a candy store.

Where should he go first?

Josephine only heard the shots because she had been listening for them. There was one shot, then a long silence as she sat hardly breathing until she heard the second one. After that she stood up and moved toward the batwing doors.

She stopped there. It took her a few seconds to become aware that the bartender, Potts, was behind her.

"You don't want to go out there," he

said gently.

"Yes," she said, "I do . . . but I won't."

She didn't want either man to be killed because each was watching out for her.

Or would either one of them even be worried about that?

CHAPTER
THIRTY-ONE

Decker, his rifle held in his left hand and resting on his shoulder, his right hand dangling by his cutdown, walked along the boardwalk on Main Street like he owned it.

The town was beginning to come to life, people walking on both sides of the street as well as in the middle, wagons clattering past, stores opening. Decker was alert for attack from either side or from the rooftops as he made his way to the livery stable. He still believed Brand wouldn't run, but now he wanted to make sure.

When he reached the livery the old man was sitting in a chair out front.

"How you doing, old-timer?"

"Fine, mister."

"And my horse?"

"Your horse is jest fine."

"That's good. Uh, you know a fella named Brand?"

"That fella that lives with Miss Josephine?"

"That's him."

"Ladies in town don't approve of that, I kin tell you," the old man said.

"I guess they wouldn't. Does he keep his horse here?"

"He sure does. It's that roan two stalls down from your gelding."

"He hasn't been here this morning, has he?"

"Nope."

"I want you to do me a favor, old-timer."

"What's that?"

"I want you to lock up for a while."

"If I lock up, folks won't be able to get their horses out."

"That's the general idea," Decker said. He took out some money. "Let's just say I'm renting the whole place for the morning, horses and all."

The old man looked at the money in his hand and said, "Yes, sir, whatever you say!"

"Go get yourself some breakfast — and make it last."

The old man stood up, padlocked the livery doors, then ambled away, counting his money.

Decker had effectively cut Brand off from his horse. Now the only way he'd get out of town was on foot or by stealing someone else's horse.

From the rooftop of the Feed and Grain, Brand saw what Decker was doing, and he admired him for it. He'd managed to lock away both of their horses, and since, at this time of the morning, there weren't that many animals on the street, Brand would have limited opportunity to steal one — not that he had any intentions of doing so. The only thing on his mind right now was getting rid of Decker.

He picked up his rifle and sighted down on the bounty hunter, who was standing in front of the locked livery. Brand knew he was a better shot with a handgun than a rifle, but he decided to give it a try, anyway.

Decker heard the shot and the sound of the bullet as it whizzed past his ear and embedded itself in the livery door. As he ducked for cover he realized that the shot was too damn close to be a deliberate miss.

Brand was playing for the whole pot now.

Decker couldn't see where the Baron was, but the highest point he could have fired from was the Feed and Grain. It afforded him the best view of the livery. That meant that Brand knew he was locked into town.

Decker moved around behind the livery,

then along the back of a block of stores in order to get to the Feed and Grain. He knew Brand would be gone by now, but it would give him a starting point.

He'd never tried to track a man through a town before, but there was a first time for everything.

Josephine heard the shot and jumped in her seat.

"That was a rifle, wasn't it?" she asked Potts.

"Sounded like it."

"Decker has a shotgun, doesn't he?"

"He does, but if he's worth his salt, he'll have his rifle with him too. That shotgun's not gonna do him much good from across the street."

"Were those shots fired from one gun or two?" Josephine demanded apprehensively.

"One, ma'am, but my guess is Decker won't fire until he knows he'll hit what he's shooting at."

"I see."

"Can I get you something else, ma'am?"

"Yes," she said. "I want another glass of whiskey."

Brand had left the roof of the Feed and Grain just moments before Decker arrived on the scene. He was in front of the building while Decker was in back.

Brand was looking around, trying to gauge his next move, when he noticed that the Broadus House was open.

Why would the saloon be open this early? he wondered.

He headed that way to find out.

Decker was on the roof of the Feed and Grain when he saw Brand go into the saloon.

"Shit!"

CHAPTER
THIRTY-TWO

When Brand entered the saloon he saw Josephine seated at a table, drinking a glass of whiskey.

"Josephine!"

She looked up and saw him, and her eyes went wide. She wasn't afraid any longer, though. She'd had very little liquor in her life, and two shot glasses had begun to make her feel giddy.

"Well, if it isn't the notorious Baron," she said, raising her glass to him. "Decker proving to be an elusive target?"

"What are you doing here?" Brand demanded. "Why aren't you at the store?"

"Don't wanna be at the store," she said. "Don't wanna be anywhere but here."

Brand moved to the table, put his rifle down, and grabbed her by the arm.

"Come on —"

"Let go!" she shouted.

"Hey!" Potts said.

Brand glared at him and said, "You stay out of this, bartender!"

"She may be your woman, Brand," Potts said, "but that ain't no way to treat her."

Potts started around the bar and Brand reacted through reflex — the reflex that had become part of the Baron's life.

He drew and fired.

Josephine watched in horror as the bullet struck Potts in the center of the chest. Potts stopped in his tracks, a puzzled look coming over his face. He opened his mouth as if to say something, and blood trickled from it.

He fell forward, dead.

"No!" Josephine shouted.

She ran and knelt by the body of the dead man, throwing an accusing look at Brand.

"You killed him!" she screamed. "You killed him for no reason!"

"I thought —" he said. "Bartenders usually have a shotgun behind the bar. I thought he was —"

"You didn't think," she said. "You just reacted the way a killer reacts. You're a killer, just like Decker said."

"Decker!" Brand shouted. "And what do you think Decker is? A saint?"

"He's an honorable man. He knows what he is and what he does and he doesn't try to hide it. He doesn't go off and kill and then come back and hide behind a woman."

"Is that what you think?" he said. "That I was hiding behind you?"

"Yes," she said. "I think you're a coward, Brand — or Baron, or whatever you call yourself! A coward, damn you!" she shouted, and she started crying.

Brand thought she was crying for the bartender or for Decker or for herself. It never occurred to him that she might be crying for him, for the man she had thought he was.

"All right," he said, looking at his rifle. "All right, then."

As if on cue, from outside came Decker's voice.

"Brand! You in there, Brand? Or did you duck out the back door?"

"I'm here," Brand called out, looking at Josephine. "I'm coming out, Decker."

Josephine looked up at him then, her face streaked with tears, and said, "Don't' —"

"Don't kill him?" he asked. "That's just what I'm going to do, Josephine. I'm going to kill him!"

As Brand went out the batwing doors, Josephine said in a low voice, "No, I mean . . . don't go."

Decker waited out in the street for Brand.
So, it would end this way after all.

CHAPTER
THIRTY-THREE

BLAM!

Josephine knew that was no rifle, that could only have been a shotgun.

"Once," she said to the dead Potts. "He fired once, just like you said."

EPILOGUE I

When Decker rode into the logging camp trailing a horse with a body slung over it, he drew a lot of attention. Dani Boone came out to meet him, as did Frenchie.

He did not see Jeff Reno.

"Decker, welcome back," Frenchie said heartily. He looked pointedly at the body on the horse and asked, "Get what you were after?"

"I did," Decker said, dismounting.

Looking anxious, Dani said, "Did he kill my father?"

"To be honest, Dani, he died before I could ask him."

She compressed her lips and then said tightly, "You mean you killed him before you could ask him."

"That's true," Decker said, "but I don't believe he did it."

"How can you —" she started, but Frenchie put his hand on her shoulder.

"Let the man talk, honey."

"Are you missing any men?" Decker asked.

"Yeah," Frenchie said, "as a matter of fact we're missing two. I understand there's also a man missing from one of the other camps. Why?"

"They trailed me and tried to kill me."

"Why would they do that?" Dani asked.

"Because they were paid to."

"By who?"

"By the man who killed your father and then tried to pin it on a professional killer called the Baron."

"Who are you talking about?" Frenchie asked.

"Who first brought up the Baron's name?"

Decker knew the answer, and as he watched Frenchie he saw the truth dawn on him, also.

"Reno."

"Jeff Reno?" Dani said. "But why?"

"Maybe he figured he'd take over once your father was dead," Decker said.

"But he didn't. I came along. Why not try to kill me?"

"He couldn't," Decker said. "He had to first find out if I was dead or if I had reached the Baron. He couldn't kill you and blame the Baron if the killer had been caught or killed himself."

"Reno," Frenchie said from between clenched teeth.

"Where is he?" Decker asked.

Dani looked at Frenchie.

"He's on the south slope," Frenchie said.

"Show me —" Decker said.

"Wait," Frenchie said. "He won't have a gun there, Decker. Let me handle it."

"Are you sure?"

Frenchie smiled a terrible smile and said, "I'm very sure."

He walked off, and a bunch of men trotted after him, not wanting to miss the fight that was sure to follow.

"Dani, Reno's pretty big —"

"Don't worry," she said. "Frenchie's never been beaten, and he won't be beaten by Jeff Reno."

"Still —"

"Come inside and have a cup of coffee," she said. "Do you want to spend the night?"

He looked at her face, but she had asked the question in total innocence, unaware of how it had sounded.

"I guess," Decker said. "I'll have to get started early in the morning, though. Do you want me to take Reno with me?"

"We heard that the marshal will be here at the beginning of the week," Dani said. "We

222

can hold Reno until then."

A man took both horses from Decker, and he followed Dani to her cabin.

"Tell the marshal I'll be glad to come back if he needs me."

She stopped at the door, and before opening it, turned and said, "How about if I need you?"

He wondered if that had been said with the same innocence as her previous remark.

EPILOGUE II

Decker pulled his horse up in front of the sheriff's office in Douglas, Wyoming. He dismounted and tied off the horse that was hauling the Baron's body.

The bounty hunter mounted the boardwalk and pounded on the door. Moments later Sheriff Calder came rushing out.

"What the hell —" he said, and then stopped short when he saw Decker.

"I brought you something," Decker said, jerking his thumb in the direction of the second horse.

Calder looked at him, then walked over to the horse and held up the dead man's head so he could see him.

"You ever meet the Baron?" Decker asked.

"Once," Calder said, studying the dead man's face.

"Is that him?" Decker asked.

Calder dropped the man's head and said, "That's him, all right. You got him."

"I got him."

"And you brought him all the way down here to me?"

"Yep," Decker said.

The sheriff mounted the boardwalk, and Decker looked him right in the eye.

"I want signing my chit for the bounty on the Baron to be your last official act as sheriff of Douglas, Wyoming."

The employees of Thorndike Press hope you have enjoyed this Large Print book. All our Thorndike, Wheeler, and Kennebec Large Print titles are designed for easy reading, and all our books are made to last. Other Thorndike Press Large Print books are available at your library, through selected bookstores, or directly from us.

For information about titles, please call:
  (800) 223-1244

or visit our Web site at:
  http://gale.cengage.com/thorndike

To share your comments, please write:
  Publisher
  Thorndike Press
  295 Kennedy Memorial Drive
  Waterville, ME 04901